THE GLASS CASTLE

**If they didn't watch out, the Glass Castle
was in for trouble – and all the good
works with it! For Ellie was to learn
"Good Works" could get you killed!**

Ellen Murphy

Part of the Lady Jane Series

1

The author thanks Jay W. Foreman for his help and expertise in getting this book published.

2

Ellen dedicates her writing to her daughters: Suzy and Kathy and in memory of her precious "Al".

List of Characters

Elizabeth "Ellie" Masters – Whose interest in helping others may get her killed

Ruth Roberts – Friend of the family and caretaker of Ellie, who finds herself in unexpected financial circumstances

Madeline Masters – Ellie's Mother who dies too young

Major Alfred Masters – Loving husband and father but missing during the war

Kenneth Thompson – Handsome friend of Ellie and one who may have his mind changed about helping people

Doctor Ormond – A physician of note and a guest - Thank Heavens!

An 1800's estate whose future owner was more concerned with the welfare of those less fortunate than her wealth or evidently her own safety!

Estates were virtual villages of people with varying jobs and skills. Some of the owners were good stewards of the land and of their staff. Many of the well to do lived interesting lives attending many events and parties in London but the main characters in this series are more interested in helping others.

Ellie is a delight and so very enthusiastic about helping people learn better ways to work and take care of themselves. She has spent huge amounts of her fortune to this avail. Her further desire to provide education to those who have not had that experience causes surprise and sometimes consternation but is definitely to the benefit of the masses.

THE GLASS CASTLE

Prologue:

Ellie (really Elizabeth Angelina Masters) liked to make up stories and fairy tales of her own, since she was a very precocious child of four.

Now a young lady of eighteen it was childish so she never let anyone know! But she still did it – at least on occasion. And for her own enjoyment only! Those fairytales had recently taken a new turn and she mused about her future and reflected on her past...her life was about to change drastically, she hoped she would make the right decisions! She had found someone she liked very much indeed – how would that turn out?

But unbeknownst to her, not only fairy tales were in her future. A ghastly deed would be experienced too! Were her good works going to get her killed? Could fairy tales really come true? Could she survive the ill will that was to come? All of these things included her home – which she dubbed her "Glass Castle."

Getting Acquainted and Growing Up Problems:

CHAPTER ONE

Ellie was a lonely child, although she did not realize it…she just thought it was normal for any almost nine-year-old to be schooled at home and not venture out for anything like picnics or entertainment. Having no young cousins, she did not even visit other children, her mother not being inclined to encourage her to make friends with others of her age at church or in the small town. They never went to London – or very, very rarely.

She had no siblings and her lovely mother, Madeline, had just died of cholera at the ripe age of thirty-one following almost a year of horrible sickness – Ellie was eight at her last birthday. Her father was a military officer and rarely home, If there was a war anywhere, he was probably in it. She did not doubt he loved her and her mother. At least he seemed to on the occasions he did make it home on leave for a week or two at a time. However, during her Mother's last illness, he was not to be located, and so Mother died without his concern and help and Ellie did not know whether to miss him or hate him for abandoning them when they needed him the most of EVER!

Thankfully, Madeline's maiden Aunt Ruth Roberts was a lovely, kind young woman, who came and sat through the awful time, assisting the hired nurse for almost ten months to keep Ellie's mother comfortable and trying her very best to make Ellie feel better and feel loved.

Ellie knew Ruth to be so generous with her time for reading aloud, wiping brows, dispensing medicine, and helping any way she could. From Ellie's standpoint she was great at aiding her to understand her arithmetic and spelling, learning to make cookies when the chef would let them mess up the kitchen and just BEING THERE when things were so scary and even an eight-year-old girl knew the outcome was not going to be good!

Aunt Ruth was quite young but had not married, having nursed both parents through traumatic illnesses instead of attending parties and events where she would have met an eligible bachelor. Ellie often wondered if Ruth was lonely.

After the inevitable funeral for Lady Madeline Aker Masters, Ellie's mother, when the house had been full of people Ellie did not know, like another aunt, Aunt Bea, who called her "Dear" and asked about her dolls! Ellie fled to "her" corner in the library. She had not played with dolls in three years. Or Lord Latimore, who came asking when he could bid on the property and Mother was still in the coffin in the library!

She was told by several people that they would be "taking care of her," which although may have been intended to be consoling, instead worried her no end! She was not naïve, even at eight, so she knew they would never let her live here with just the servants, that considerable money was in trust from her Mother's parents, and that their ideas of "help" were self-served! But she did not at all want to go with anyone unless it was Aunt Ruth!

As to the sale of the property, although very young and rarely talked to like an adult, her mother three weeks ago, while still able to speak coherently, had assured her this would be her home until she could decide at twenty-one what she wanted to do. It would not be sold! Well now, there was something….she would decide? Mother also had told her not to worry about where she would live or who would take care of her. Not worry? Her mother should see this group…well she hoped her mother was correct. How interesting. How alarming!

Several relatives, who had not lifted a hand to help during the many months of illness, came forward with all kinds of fake attempts to console the "Dear Child" and offered to take her, but she resisted.

She had watched from her corner as the undertaker had sealed up the coffin and she had followed obediently when it was taken to the family burial ground in the back. Aunt Ruth close beside her but thankfully not "hovering." She had closed her eyes during the burial, however. She knew what they did but she could not watch it. Maybe, she would regret that later but doubted it. A few relatives remained until that was done, but none approached her further.

Finally, returning to the den, an abbreviated portion of her Mother's last will was read by the attorney, and hallelujah, it said Aunt Ruth was to have custody and the payment per month of a sufficient sum that would more than take care of Ellie's keep and schooling until she came into her inheritance at 21. Also, no large bequests were made to any of the hovering relatives. This seemed fair to Ellie, after all they hadn't lifted a hand to help, sit with her Mother, read to her Mother, or do anything at all for Ellie, the sad and lonely child, in the long months Lady Madeline Masters had been ill. And for Ellie over the years, not even a card or small present at Christmas or her birthday! Of course, Aunt Ruth had always sent notes and presents to her <u>and</u> her mother…interesting things…like books, plays, and pictures. Even sending Ellie a small pearl necklace on her eighth birthday…she prized it more than ANYTHING!

When everyone had gone, some with great consternation, the attorney, Sir Edward Ambrose, came over. He announced that Aunt Ruth would have the choice of living at her current residence or living rent free at the property currently used by Ellie. If she chose her own home, Ellie, for security sake would need to go with her but they could both live here for certain. After all, this property was now owned by Ellie, but in trust so she couldn't sell it until she was of age. They were both speechless. Ellie thought: Was he serious? She would so love to live here! Not that there was anything wrong with Aunt Ruth's house, but it was small in comparison with little yard and here she had the huge lawn, the animals (horses, cows, pigs and cats), and room to move.

Aunt Ruth looked at her and smiled, reading her mind. Aunt Ruth asked the attorney – "What about my house if I choose to live for a time in this one?"
"Well, Ma'am, you may keep it and rent it out, loan it to a relative, or anything else reasonable you wish. It is yours, of course, and not involved in this will. It is advised that you not sell it because if Elizabeth leaves here, then you must too, because this never becomes your house – only yours to use while you are with Elizabeth."

"Isn't this a rather unusual will, Sir?" asked Aunt Ruth.

"Yes, indeed it is rather and I took quite a time researching and making certain the designation was correct and not subject to overthrow if appealed. However, I did determine, that while rare it is accepted in law. So yes, you and Elizabeth may live here, it can be done should that be your decision.

You, Ruth Roberts, are the one who makes the determination and signs off on it as you are officially the guardian for Elizabeth also in this will, but I assume you will consult with her. Now Major Masters, when he returns from the war, may live here as long as it is acceptable to Elizabeth and you until she is of age and can make her own choices. He likewise will not own it. Please take the rest of this week – four days and come to my office on Monday at ten in the morning, both of you. My address is on the paperwork and we will make things official and sign all necessary papers at that time. Now, we will not hurry you if there is an issue to be researched but can get it finalized quickly if not, it is quite explicit and true to her habit, Lady Masters had studied and decided all questions very well! Does that sound agreeable?"

"Yes, Sir, it does indeed, we will both be there Monday and let you know. Oh, another question. It has not been possible to reach Elizabeth's father during this terrible time, what of him? Does he have no rights to this property?"

"No, he has no interest in it at all. There is a fund in the joint names of Captain Masters and the late Lady Masters that will be entirely his now and is specifically listed as NOT being part of this estate in Mrs. Master's will. There is also a specific bequest to him as there is to you. However as to all the real estate and its attachments, the very large financial investments and deposits, and so forth that are specifically in Mrs. Masters will, are to continue the title as it had been for years – passing only to children of the deceased. It does not automatically include their spouses or their progeny until death requires a change or underage children inherit upon reaching majority of 21 years.

Such do have the use of the property from date of the death of the owner, if properly chaperoned and protected for those years. You qualify as proper chaperone and protector, Madam, and of course Elizabeth is the only child involved. Now, that said, when Elizabeth does achieve maturity, she may change those provisions in her own will. Anything her Mother has decreed now will only apply until Elizabeth is twenty-one, at which time she may change it if she wants to but does not have to do so….it will continue on as stated now unless she does make an official change and put it on record less than thirteen years from now."

"The only other specification, you and Elizabeth may decide, is if anyone else, other than staff you hire, may live here. That would include her father, a husband of yours should you marry, any children of yours, a husband of Elizabeth's if she marries before reaching her majority according to the will which is 21 years and so forth. You are quite young yet Miss Roberts and it is not unforeseeable that you would marry, in which case this could be your home with that husband – while Elizabeth is here that is."

"Well, you certainly have given us a lot to think about. One other thing, the money provided for Elizabeth's care, as inferred at the reading today, is that all the money available? It is the only figure of which I am familiar. This is a large estate and such things as a roof or chimney could easily use a good portion of the maintenance. What then?"
"You are very wise and I was going to address that on Monday, but so you don't fret and to help your decision making, there is a very, very large fund that attaches to this property that can be used for improvements, repairs or furniture for use on this property only. In addition, the property itself generates good money that is regularly added to those funds but not as restricted, such as the sale of

cattle or horses, farm and edible products raised on the property, rental of two tenant houses and so forth. The other properties in the estate also have their own maintenance funds and currently have excellent managers, who were trusted by Lady Masters.

They are extremely lucrative and have separate financial funds of which you and Elizabeth will be informed at another time. You and Elizabeth would be quite comfortable here. Such money as from the cattle and produce are also available for regular purchases such as household goods, foods, medicines, clothing, any expenses to keep proper staff including wages and any benefits you declare.

You should know that the will allows for payment of any expenses of those allowed to reside here in addition to Elizabeth's allowance. It is also decreed that any interest earned on the large holdings can be used as well for household matters or for the benefit of Elizabeth with my approval – and anything reasonable would not be questioned. Such funds could be school, tutor, or university fees, medical things of note including surgeries and attendants, replacement furniture, clothing, concerts, travel, a small addition such as a sunroom or back porch, repairs anywhere on the property, any number of items if not specifically denied in the documents. Such denials being few and far between.

The funds generate and earn quite a generous amount of such monies. Full maintenance can be maintained, almost anything you can imagine would be approved. Security, farm workers, and household staff of many varieties can be hired. Again, that includes payment of such expenses for anyone living on the property also such as you both, a husband of yours Miss Roberts, and Major Masters.

True to her nature, Elizabeth (Ellie), sat quietly and waited for the meeting to be over. She was astounded at the money involved and that she could have things like a piano, which her mother had refused saying she was too young. Of course, she is young for Heaven's sake she is only eight, well almost nine,…but oh, to have a piano and piano lessons….wouldn't that be marvelous!

Staff had finally gotten the hangers-on to leave the premises and once Sir Edward left, Ellie heard Aunt Ruth sigh. Well, she understood. What a list of things to consider and after giving up her home for the over eight months she had helped here, wouldn't Aunt Ruth want to go back to her own house? Could she think of this as "home"? Ellie had not been in Aunt Ruth's house in two years but remembered it as being small in comparison to this huge mansion but still very lovely. The flower garden, vegetable garden and small lawn were beautifully cared for and the house itself was so comforting….one could sit on nicely upholstered furniture in any room and food and beverages were not limited to the tearoom or dining room like here.

Ellie really loved Aunt Ruth's house for visiting, however this was her home and although the house was cold and formal, the grounds were where Ellie spent her time. Even when she was studying and reading, which she did remarkably well for her age. As frequently as possible, she was outside or in one of the barns usually, except of course in the later days of her Mother's illness.

"Well, Ellie, dear, what say we have our tea and see if Suzanne has prepared any treats for us. The food at the funeral was fine but not appealing to me and I noticed you did not take any either…come child, let us see what we can find."

"Aunt Ruth," asked Ellie with a mouth full of raisin biscuits, her favorite, "can I have a piano now?"

Ruth Roberts grinned all over herself. She had wondered how long it would take the child to request one. She knew it had been denied by the girl's mother more than once but thought it an excellent idea. The child was so bright and would learn quickly, she was certain.

"Well, Missy, why don't we look at some on Monday after the meeting with Sir Ambrose. There is a store near to his office and we can see what looks good. They also will probably know of a teacher who

17

would agree to come to the estate to give you lessons!"

She was unprepared for the immediate hug and kiss, complete with biscuit crumbs! Laughing and wiping her cheek, she said: "Careful, don't choke on the food. I take that as a "Yes" and we will plan to do so. If the attorney takes an inordinate amount of time we can have luncheon in a tearoom on the same block as the piano store. This afternoon, or what is left of it, why don't we decide where such a piano should be placed? That would give staff time to move furniture or whatever.

May I suggest it be somewhere that light can come in at your back to make reading the music easier than by candlelight. You decide on locations we can explore; this is your house and I want you to be satisfied with the piano's placement. It will be quite large and need a lot of space and not near a bedroom where you might disturb a sleeper if you practice quite early or late."

Ellie was surprised! "Her house?" Well, by golly, yes it is, but she had never considered it so. She rarely even thought of it as "home".

Her Mother was very lovely and quite nice but had many rules. One was that she was a child and had no opinions....well evidently that was to change. Huh! If it turned out to be so, she would like that very much. She knew she was just a child but she did have ideas on things, at least she would like to express them on occasion, even if overruled!

Ellie looked at the empty plate and tea pot. She had never been asked to help staff, but always worried that they had to be at the beck and call of her Mother. Now, Mother was not mean or anything, but why in the name of common sense did they never take their dirty dishes to the kitchen or put anything away? She could not figure it out. She proceeded to put all the leavings of their tea onto the tray and very, very carefully started toward the kitchen with the load.

Aunt Ruth saw her and came, relieving her of the big teapot. Well, a clever idea, the whole thing was cumbersome and heavier than she had thought. Aunt Ruth did not say a thing but held the door open for her and together they returned the tea things to a very, very surprised kitchen staff. They bowed to her and she giggled and returned the bow, taking Aunt Ruth's hand and leading her out onto the back lawn. At first Ruth was going to ignore the action and then changed her mind. "That was very thoughtful of you, Dear."

Ellie giggled again and said, "Well, they wait on me all the time, and I don't feel it hurts to do a little favor for them once in a while."

Ellie announced that the piano should go in the study, with the big glass doors that looked out on the back

19

lawn. The double-door would provide enough light in the daytime and the study was not beneath the bedrooms. Plus, the large candle chandelier hanging from the center of the ceiling would give evening light as well. Ruth said that was an excellent idea and was so pleased that Ellie had figured the whole thing out herself – and quickly too.

Aunt Ruth asked, "Ellie, have you ever wanted a pet of any kind? I appreciate how nice you are with the horses and cows and pet the barn cats. Would you like a puppy to train and go places with you?"

Ellie looked at her like she had two heads. "Are you serious Aunt Ruth? Can I have a pet? A kitten or a puppy?"

"Why, yes Dear, I believe it would be very good for you to have something to take care of and for it to be good to you as well. Either a kitten or puppy would be fine with me, but only if you want one and will help with its care."

"Oh, Aunt Ruth, what a lovely idea! Do you have a minute right now? May I show you the kitten I have been playing with in the barn? I did not dare bring it to the house and upset Mother, but it comes as soon as I enter the stable area. Big Jim says it kills the mice that get in the horse feed, so he keeps cats. This one kitten is very friendly to me though. Some run from you but this one doesn't."

Ellie thought – what an outstanding day this was. Great sorrow of course, her Dear Mother had passed but that was mixed feelings, the last weeks all her Mother had done was groan – not eating, drinking, or talking at all and so very, very miserable. She would miss her Mother forever and ever but knew she was not hurting now and that in itself was a relief. She had been in so much pain for the best part of a year and could not eat or drink lately – it was awful to watch. In the end she did not even looked like Mother, her cheeks sunken in and her skin all gray even her bones looked like they would puncture the skin for lack of tissue. The last two weeks she had not responded to any talk except to moan.

She felt a tear roll down her cheek and wiped it away quickly. She had loved her Mother very much, but she was so stern about everything Ellie wanted to do....no pet, no piano lessons, any schoolwork redone. Plus, she was never taken to the city to see any sights or anything. When she grew up, if she had children, however that came about, she would explain things to them and not make so many rules!

Ellie took Ruth's hand and led her into the area where "Big Jim," really James Smith, was busy cleaning horse hooves. When he looked up and saw Ellie, his smile was wide. He came and bowed to both ladies and expressed his sorrow to Ellie about her mother. She thanked him with a bit of a quaver in her voice and then asked if Jimbo, the kitten was around. Jim grinned broadly and pointed behind her. As she turned the kitten wound around her legs. "He heard you Miss Ellie. See he comes to say 'Hello'".

Ellie immediately sat down on a bale of straw and the kitten jumped into her lap. It was hard to tell if the kitten or Ellie was happier!

"James," said Ellie, "can we take the kitten into the house? I promise to take real good care of it!"

"Well, Miss Ellie, it is not for me to decide. Miss Ruth will have to make that decision and we will need to prepare a box for it to sleep in, a box for it to do its business – which will need to be cleaned every day, and it will need a small plate and two bowls – one for water and one for milk, probably set on a tray or rag rug to catch any mess. Do you think you can prepare all that?"

"Oh, I already have most of that in my closet. Asking staff what would be needed if I ever got Mother to agree to a kitten and they have helped me find what would work. The dishes may need to be washed because it has been a long, long, time since I planned it. Probably at least three months. But it is there. Miss Amy, my maid knows about it but she never told on me. She said it did no harm in the closet so she did not make me move it.

Ruth had to turn away because she was crying. The poor baby, no piano, no pet, her time regimented between reading schoolbooks and the bible – neither being bad but an eight-year-old girl needed somewhat else certainly?

She heard Big Jim clear his throat and turned, trying to get herself under control. She gave him a wavering smile and said she would check on the things in the bedroom and if satisfactory, they would be back tomorrow morning to get the kitten.

Ellie clapped her hands and laughed. She did not holler with glee as another child would have, after all she was raised by Madeline Aker Masters and would have been lectured on self-control from a baby.

"Oh, James, pardon me, but is there a riding horse on Ellie's property that would be suitable for her to ride? I learned to ride before I was five years old and she is now past eight so she could easily sit a horned saddle. She could learn to ride side saddle later, but a horned saddle is much easier to learn on."

"Oh, Ma'am, I agree with you. Yes, let us see her now. We won't ride her today," he said looking directly at Ellie. "But we will clean her up and there is a small saddle from when your Mother learned to ride in the tack room. We will oil it and make certain it is in good repair, but to answer again: "Yes, indeed we can get you riding. Would you also wish to ride when she does, Ruth?"

"Oh, Jim, not being in a saddle for some time I will be rusty but I would love to ride. If you have a gentle beast, who will not toss me into a pond, I would be so pleased to ride with her. We will check with you tomorrow on the kitten and look about helping to clean the leathers for riding." She said, winking at him when she mentioned the cleaning of the leathers. Well, good for her, he thought. She would show the girl the proper way to care for her things and not put everything off on staff as her mother had done. They approached the horse and Ellie looked askance but after Ruth and Big Jim stroked it she got the courage to do the same. The horse looked at her and bowed his head for further petting. She was thrilled!

Jim had liked Lady Masters well enough but like all staff was always conscious that she felt she was far above them and she should never do any tasks at all. He often wondered what she did do with her time besides read and embroider. She did not ride horses, work in the flower garden, take the child to town for enjoyment, buy and play the pianoforte, or even hardly ever attend a concert or recitation. It must have been boring and lonely for her but of her own choosing.

They all knew the Master was seldom home, being an Army man who stayed in the service although they felt he had sufficient years to retire from it. Perhaps there was nothing on the estate he wished to do, but it was a shame for the child. Staff had been concerned lately when they knew a search for him had not turned up a result. What if he was killed in battle and the family not notified?

Ruth and Ellie had a nice dinner together, not in the cold huge dining room, but in the glassed porch on the small table where they could watch rabbits in the yard and birds too. Ellie was very surprised at dinner. How did they know what she liked? She had never been allowed to request any special meals, but there was roasted chicken, peas, and creamed potatoes. All favorites of hers. Plus, there was dessert. When Mother ordered dinner she only allowed dessert on Sundays or special days like birthdays or company. Ellie had gotten the kitchen staff to make the creamed potatoes after Aunt Ruth had brought some to the house...delicious.

The dessert was caramel flan. She knew, if allowed, she could eat the whole plate full, but she did not take more than two pieces. She watched a couple pretty birds, ignoring the table, and when she turned around a third piece of flan was on her plate. She looked at Aunt Ruth and got a wink. She immediately ate the whole piece. She was so full! She did not usually feel so full after a meal, nothing being desirable enough for extra helpings, but today...well today she felt she had enough to eat and it was all delicious.

She hopped up and ran to the kitchen to tell them all how great the dinner was. Little did she realize but the kitchen ladies cried when she left the room.

Ruth went to her as she looked out the window and said, "Darling, I believe we should maybe walk out to the grave again. It is the day of the burial and I don't want you to regret later that maybe you didn't pay homage enough to your Dear Mother."

Solemnly nodding her head, she reached for Ruth's hand and together they walked across the yard to the fenced in cemetery where so many relatives were buried. Staff had carefully covered the mound, using sod previously removed and placed the many flower arrangements on top. The stone had not returned from being chiseled but it was a nice and neat place. Ellie sobbed as she knelt beside her mother and Ruth cried also, for the poor sick woman, who abided by her strict upbringing all her life and had so little joy and so little camaraderie with her lovely daughter. What a shame. She promised God that she would do better by the child and asked her niece for forgiveness for doing so.

After a bit she felt a little hand in hers and they walked back to the house silently.

Both were exhausted and with silent but mutual agreement went upstairs to their respective bedrooms. Neither felt they wanted more food they told the staff. Having eaten the lovely dinner by huge helpings. Ruth helped Ellie undo the buttons of her plain dark blue dress and hang it in the far back corner of her closet. There was a tub of warm water already placed in the adjoining bath area and Ellie's maid, Amy, came in and helped her wash and get into the nightgown she had chosen to wear.

Ruth returned in her own nightgown and robe. She hugged her and said they would get the saddle, bridle and other horse gear clean and oiled tomorrow so they could ride the next day and also bring out the kitten things and maybe bring the little fellow into the house to see how he would fare living somewhere other than the barn.

On these happy notes, Ellie was smiling, reaching up to encircle Ruth's neck and kiss her firmly on the cheek a third time. Ruth tucked her in but did not realize the child got back up and brought out the kitten things from the closet, ready for the new tenant the next day.

Ruth had trouble getting to sleep. She rarely did but tonight there were several things rolling around in her mind that she couldn't quiet. She was most concerned about taking care of Elizabeth. The child would be more wealthy than anyone else she had ever known…even more wealthy than Madeline because the estate coming to her would gain untold additional income from earnings and interest so would quickly surpass the amount Elizabeth would inherit. It was bound to attract unwanted attention. Not just people trying to get acquainted either for a handout or for things Elizabeth could provide them....but ner'do'wells too!   Elizabeth would be the object of unscrupulous people and events. How to protect her? Of course, they would take great care to not make her wealth public, but it would be dangerous for the child to venture out. However, they couldn't keep her cloistered here...it was not fair to her to be hidden away as her mother had been. Oh, Dear! Well, she would do her best of course.

She didn't want Ellie to be scared and would carefully train her about not discussing the estate or her income, but Ruth would also see Ellie had protection if possible.

CHAPTER TWO

Ellie noted what an enjoyable day it was going to be
to get outside. Now, thankfully it was Thursday and
the funeral behind them. She had heard staff cleaning
the rooms where Mother had been so ill and
removing all evidence of the funeral in the parlor.
Ruth had gone down quite early for a cup of tea and
looked out the pretty windows at the birds and
squirrels. She heard a noise and there was Ellie,
already dressed in an everyday frock with only one
petticoat, obviously ready to tackle the work in the
barn. They had an early and brief breakfast then
rushed toward the horse stable before the sun was
fully up.

Big Jim was yawning and finishing a mug of coffee
when he was surprised to hear the feminine voices in
the tack room. Peeking in he saw a very excited Ellie
holding a small dirty saddle close to her body with
both hands. Quite a heavy burden for such a small
girl but she was grinning all over herself and a still
sleepy looking Ruth was showing her how to place it
on the saddle stand where she could reach it to use
the saddle soap and buff it clean.

"Good morning, Jim! We made ourselves at home in
your barn. If you will show us where more rags are

we will get to work....this young lady is so enthusiastic she woke me before it was fully light. Once we are started, feel free to finish your repast if we have interrupted you."

"I will be glad to help, Ruth, I have eaten with my wife and this is my second cup so I am ready to tackle the tackle." Ellie laughed as intended and took the rag from him, wetting it in a small bucket and rubbing it generously with the saddle soap. He prepared one as well and showed her how to rub in circles, wipe with a dry piece of cloth and then rub a second time or until the rag looked clean. It took a while, the saddle not having been used in many years, but they all helped and finally had a very pretty, if damp saddle. He was impressed that Ellie was concentrating on getting all the little creases and edges. He bragged on her thorough job and she giggled.

He showed her how to take it out to the fence and place it across one of the wider boards out of the sun, but in the fresh air to dry better than the towels had done. He explained too much sun on the wet leather may make it dry too quickly and crack.

Being a very bright girl and enthusiastic, Ellie was starting on the reins, stirrups, and breast straps. What a good girl she was. He was surprised how hard she worked, knowing things had been done for her all her eight years past.

By mid-morning they had the equipment cleaned and polished with leather soap which was really not only a cleaner but a finishing product as well, he explained. Ellie learned you should not ride until the leather was dry from its bath. Ruth suggested that they go back to the house for nourishment and take the kitten with them to see how it would react to the house. Ellie thanked Big Jim without being prompted, which he and Ruth noticed, and with the kitten in her arms they headed back to the house.

After entering the house, Ellie had laughed until her sides hurt, just watching Jimbo explore. He did not miss a thing, smelling, and scooting under chairs, and behind bookcases – until she was afraid he would get stuck. Then he would surprise her by coming out the other side. She finally picked him up and took him to her room. Unbeknownst to her, Amy had put milk and water in the dishes, obviously now clean and a small portion of feed that they had for the kitchen cats who kept mice out of the pantry.

She had not even realized it was time for nuncheon, until Aunt Ruth came and asked if she wasn't hungry? "Oh, yes, Ma'am. I am indeed quite hungry but hadn't given it a thought." Aunt Ruth laughed and said well how about putting little Jimbo in his basket on his rag rug blanket and in the closet with the doors closed so he would not have the opportunity to explore too far until more used to things. Ellie did so and had his box of dirt and bowls of water and food in there as well – still the organized little girl even though only eight years old. She watched a minute as the kitten worked his feet in the rag rug at the bottom of the basket and then laid down and went to sleep.

They dutifully washed their hands and went downstairs. Nuncheon was again a lot of foods she liked quite well. There was a casserole of potatoes and ham pieces in a nice gravy, sliced tomatoes, strawberries in cream and sugar, and a glass of cold milk. Just lovely. She told the girl waiting on them with a big smile and "Thank you!," milk mustache notwithstanding.

After eating and, of course, taking the dishes to the kitchen, to the continued amazement of staff, they went up to check on Jimbo. As she opened the door, he cowered in the basket corner and hissed, until he realized who it was and then took a big jump and landed in her lap where she sat cross-legged on the floor. He wound around her body and put his little claws in her dress to climb up to her face. She gently removed him but pet him a lot. Aunt Ruth suggested taking him to the yard and they could watch him play in the grass. Ruth pulled a ball of twine out of her pocket for the purpose and showed Ellie how to attract him by drawing it through the grass or holding it up for him to jump. A good bit of the afternoon was taken up with cat play.

Suddenly Ellie looked at Aunt Ruth with a horrified expression. "What is the matter, Dear, is somewhat amiss?"

"Oh, I haven't thanked you, I haven't said a word to you about how wonderful you are!"

"Oh, Sweetheart, there is no need. Just seeing your enjoyment is enough. And you did thank me this morning."

"No, it certainly isn't enough, Aunt Ruth. You went with me to the cemetery yesterday when I was afraid to go alone, you helped Mother for weeks upon weeks, you have helped me clean tack for riding a horse and above all else have allowed me a kitten. And I do not ignore the fact that the meals have been things I like – which I would imagine was your idea as well. I do thank you and love you, Aunt Ruth!" she said with a sob.

Hugging her, Aunt Ruth said: "Alright, now you have said it. Thank you, too, for your consideration. I love you as well. Now we have that out of the way. You do not need to thank me for each thing we do, like piano playing, and you do not need to thank me overmuch. It is my immense pleasure and we will consider this thank you to be for any future thank you how about that?"

They looked up as a shadow fell on them and Big Jim was there. "Ladies, how would it be if we saddled a horse for each of you in a little bit. Being a nice clear day, the tack seems dry and I have curried a couple horses that I think will be just the thing. There is sufficient time before supper, since this is a first-time ride. Now, you will curry your own horses sometimes, when I am too busy, but I did them for you today. Are you ready for a ride? I can take the kitten to the barn for the afternoon, where he is used to living and if your skirts are not too heavy, you could ride a while."

Since neither of them had put on extra petticoats, knowing they would be in the barn and with the kitten, they immediately stood up, nodding, and smiling at him.

Jim led them into the front of the barn and there he had two horses in the small corral. One was slightly smaller, an older mare with a few gray hairs around her face, but a gentle expression and huffing like she was greeting them.

Ellie walked toward her very slowly looking a little alarmed. Aunt Ruth went with her and showed her how to extend her hand for the horse to sniff it and then to gently stroke the nose and side of the neck in the direction of the horsehair. Then Ruth did the same to the larger animal. Both horses made soft noises at the attention and Ruth was convinced they were friendly, although she would not have doubted Big Jim's choice in any case.

Jim took both leads and encouraged the horses around in circles a few times in the corral. Ellie was still looking a little alarmed although she had been to the barn and near horses frequently, somehow, though, successfully mounting one seemed dangerous and scary, very scary. Big Jim produced a mounting block, had her step up on its first step, examined her boots for sturdiness and declared her ready to mount. She was obviously shaking but being brave and wanting very much to do this, she stepped up the next steps and putting her left foot into the stirrup as he directed. She found that it was as high as her waist. He gave her a boost and she swung her other leg over the saddle and she was up! As frightened as she was she just had to grin a little…she was amazed it was that easy.

Aunt Ruth used the mounting block as well, stating it had been half a lifetime since she rode. And she too was soon in the saddle. Jim encouraged Ruth to gently tap her heels against the side of "Honey" and make a clucking noise, see if she did not step off. Sure, and certain the horse did move out a little bit. Gently using her heels, she tapped the horse again and it moved forward a dozen or so additional steps, looking back at her as if to ask was that what she wanted? Laughing she encouraged Ellie to do the same.

Jim then assured Ellie he would not leave her side this trip, but she should do likewise, and with that motion the effect was the same just as Honey had

35

taken a few small steps, her horse, whose name was Daisy, also took steps at the command. She giggled and following instructions hanging on tightly to both the reins and saddle horn. Then tried it again, with the same result as Ruth.

Poor Jim got a workout. They both were enjoying it so much, such a change to their normal household routine. Much clicking with tongues and holding tight and giggling ensued. It must have been an hour or more that they exercised Jim and two horses. Ellie got more comfortable with each few steps and then learned how to get the horse to turn by pulling on the reins right (stating "Gee") or left (calling "Haw"), and how to get her to stop by pulling straight back and giving that command of "halt". She was riding a horse. Actually, riding a horse!

She looked down at Jim and smiled. "Thank you so much, you are wonderful to do this for us. I am having the best of times!" The big guy looked like he could cry but drew in a shaky breath and thanked her, it was his pleasure he said.

Finally, realizing that they had monopolized Jim enough, Aunt Ruth said it was time to dismount, put the gear away, curry the horses, put them in stalls to feed, and for them to head back to the house.

Ellie was amazed that she had not realized how much work was involved but gladly did her share and was not treated any differently by Aunt Ruth or Big Jim, just expected to put things away and so forth.

Jimbo came up to her and meowed like he knew he was going back to the house, so Ellie scooped him up, thanked Big Jim again for the umpteenth time, and they walked back.

Washing their hands thoroughly, they went down to eat. Tonight's dinner was pork chops. She loved pork chops! They did not often eat pork since their farm had not raised hogs until recently, but boy she loved chops and had ham the day before – how nice. There were sweet potatoes in honey glaze and more fresh berries, and asparagus, which she was learning to like but not her favorite. However, she noticed Aunt Ruth putting something on the asparagus. When she inquired, Ruth passed the pitcher and she poured the same sauce on hers and oh, it made it so much better. She was told it was called mayonnaise and was made with eggs and cream…well it was really good and helped the asparagus.

After starting the day early and having a very active time of it, Ellie admitted she was tired so she and Ruth headed up to bed. Amy helped Ellie get into her nightshirt, turn back the bed and saying her prayers. Aunt Ruth came in also ready for bed and the two hugged and Ruth got her covered and kissed her cheek. Ellie mumbled another thank you for the wonderful day and was asleep instantly.

CHAPTER THREE

Ellie was musing about Aunt Ruth. She had never encountered anyone like her, of course she had never met very many people anyway. But Aunt Ruth, she would guess, was better than most. Certainly, better than the ones she had to put up with at the funeral!

Aunt Ruth never asked for anything for herself and seemed to enjoy Ellie's having as much fun as possible. How did anyone get to be so understanding? How had SHE, Elizabeth, been so lucky as to have Aunt Ruth for a guardian? Silently, Elizabeth thanked her mother.

They had done nothing to just please Aunt Ruth. Maybe a Jane Austin novel, she had not been allowed to read one when her mother did.

It was Sunday evening and they had done bible readings that morning, deciding not to go to the local church yet. She heard a thump from the study and hurried to see what was going on. Well, she guessed she had caused all this commotion.. She went in the room cautiously.

"Good evening, Miss Elizabeth, I am sorry if we disturbed you. Although it is Sunday, we thought we would move a bit of furniture in here to make room for your piano. It is doubtful they will bring it the same day it is purchased, but we had some time this evening. Tomorrow being wash day, we would probably not have the time. Will it be all right to put it here almost in the middle of the room, do you think?"

Well, tarnation, she was being consulted? "Yes, Ma'am, that indeed would be quite all right and it is close enough to the double doors for light on my music. And under the chandelier for evening if staff will light the wicks. But I did not realize how big it would be and you have had to move that heavy desk. I am sorry to cause so much trouble."

They grinned broadly. "Oh, Miss Elizabeth, it is no trouble at all, we look forward to you playing music for us….this house is very quiet and we will enjoy it." Ellie grinned broadly, "You may not enjoy it over much in the beginning. I have never played and it might be a painful experience for your ears…but I will try really hard to learn quickly and save you as much pain as possible." and she laughed again.

The following morning Ellie and Aunt Ruth were dressed for town when they came down to breakfast. Ellie was too concerned and excited to eat much but managed to drink her milk and eat some toasted bread and blueberries with sugar. Ellie liked toasting bread by laying on the flat iron top of the kitchen stove. Amy stopped by their table and said she would look about the kitten while Ellie was gone to see if he needed to go out or had enough food. Ellie thanked her several times.

The carriage ride to town with Horace driving was a wonderful experience. Seeing all the other houses and yards was nice and passing other carriages and nodding heads to acknowledge them was new to her. There was so much to see! Some of the houses had big urns of flowers growing right by the front doors and she mentioned to Aunt Ruth how nice that looked. Aunt Ruth told her, now that it was her house, she could do the same, if she decided she wanted to. When they got home, they would find Henry, who took care of the small plants, yard and general outside work and ask him how to go about creating such a display. "You might want to notice the colors and decide what you would like so you can let Henry know – pinks, reds, yellows, white, even purple should be available." Ellie nodded, too amazed that she could do such a thing to even comment.

They passed little rows of shops, some with pastries in the window, a couple that Aunt Ruth said were taverns, where men could get a drink or bite to eat at night and those traveling could sleep. They started passing town houses and apartment buildings. How crowded it must be to live in one of those. When getting close to the attorney's office, Aunt Ruth asked her to watch for places they might eat nuncheon after the meeting.

Not long after seeing the tea rooms, they arrived at the tall building with the lawyers name, Sir Edward

Ambrose, Esquire on the brass plate attached to the building. Amazing, he had an entire building? She asked Aunt Ruth and got a wink. "Yes, Dear, he is quite successful and has several other attorneys that work for him. There will be a receptionist and secretaries and we will be escorted to his own office. Your Mother was very wise. When picking an attorney, you do not look at his charges but at his reputation and skill. You want the best to assure that your wishes are properly carried out and in the event a court case of any kind arises, you have an expert attorney to represent you."

She felt a little nervous at such an unusual process but watched Aunt Ruth and that lady did not seem nervous at all. Looking down at Ellie, Aunt Ruth said: "Don't be nervous, Dear. Remember we are his clients and will pay him. It is up to him to give us good, and faithful service, or we can find another attorney. As his clients we will be accepted with honor and it will be up to him to answer our questions and serve us....not the other way around."

My goodness, she was really getting a lot of information. She was in charge? Aunt Ruth had to be kidding. She was just a girl and Mother had often told her she did not know anything yet. Aunt Ruth reached over and patted her hand. "Not to worry, Dear, just ask any questions you wish....remember – he is working for **you**. You are the client. I am here to help you too. And I will advise when necessary, but I want you to be involved because it is your money."

They had no more than entered, what Aunt Ruth called the vestibule, and a man approached wearing a very elegant jacket, embroidered vest, white pantaloons, and shiny boots.

"Miss Roberts and Miss Masters, please follow me, Lord Ambrose is in his office and expecting you." He led them up three flights of broad stairs.

Ellie's butterflies were back in her stomach and she clutched Aunt Ruth's hand tightly. Aunt Ruth looked down at her and winked. Well, that helped.

"Good morning, Ladies! Come in! Take one of these chairs in front of my desk. Staff have provided tea and cakes if you wish. My secretary will be in soon and we will begin our discussion.

Aunt Ruth asked Ellie if she wished any tea and cakes and she said "No, thank you." She knew she could not swallow anything at all.

The office they were in had huge dark wood furniture and was at least as big as their ball room. There were two large desks and row upon row of bookcases all filled with leather bound volumes, some with gold lettering on the backs. The carpet on the floor was thick and everything quiet.

"My scribe will be in shortly; he is preparing some papers for you to peruse. He will remain and make notes of our conversation and any decisions made today. I do not want to rush you, so please know if there is something you wish to think over or discuss with someone else, just say so. You do not need to make any final decisions today, but I will be providing you with information on the laws, the monies available and some processes that will need to be followed, depending on things you decide. Miss Elizabeth, you are quite young, but Ms. Roberts has assured me you are quite astute, so your opinion will be asked. However, do not feel you need to decide too quickly, all will be explained to you until you understand. We all realize this is quite unexpected and new for you."

Elizabeth nodded and managed a weak smile.

"Here, Ms. Roberts and Ms. Masters, I have prepared some numbers for you with which to acquaint yourself. The titles of each fund are at the top of each journal. The annual allowed withdrawal of any single fund will be the next figure, clearly marked. If no such amount is shown or marked then that fund is to be used at your discretion without restriction, but of course you will be expected to use care and consideration. Now, I am certain you shall, Lady Masters had the greatest faith in you, but I must state all the rules while we talk. You will be given copies of all paperwork I present today to take with you and peruse."

Ruth did not know what she had expected, well, she did but it was not what was the reality! She had never in her life seen so much money or imagined it. She was well aware that Madeline was wealthy, having inherited the Aker monies and the whole estate spoke of affluence and good management plus there were several other properties…but this was beyond anything she could have imagined even in dreams! There were a couple of industries, a shipping company, another large farm plus the house they were living in and all its many acres and its own farming revenue.

What a huge responsibility! It would be essential that Ellie received the very best education possible to prepare her to oversee such huge wealth as would come to her. Ruth was certain not even a small fraction of all of this would be spent while the child was in her minority. In fact, maybe none of the principal would be spent with so much gathering interest. She would see Ellie learned about it all.

The paperwork included some bequests that had been made, obviously after Madeline knew she was very ill. One of the amounts was to her husband, it was more money than Ruth had enjoyed her whole life even though her parents had left her very comfortably provided for. It was not marked as distributed, so Major Masters evidently didn't know about it. The next amount she read had her looking up with alarm at the attorney. He was grinning broadly obviously watching as her fingers ran down the page. "Ah, I see you have found your distribution. It is my suggestion that you take that as soon as you can conveniently arrange for its handling, Miss Roberts. I discussed this with Madeline just before her last birthday, when she already knew she was dying and had already made Elizabeth your ward. It should make your future secure if reasonably managed and would allow you to have some luxury, such as a home at Bath or a larger estate where you could have horses."

"But I did not expect anything, My Lord. She had said I would get recompense for taking care of Elizabeth, and I assumed you would tell me of some sort of wages this morning, although I would do without it, of course, and had adamantly told her so. She had laughed at me at the time – now I see why! My parents left me my house and an annual income – maybe between 5 and 10 percent of this though. In all consciousness I cannot accept such an amount, My Lord. It is excessive in the extreme. I wished nothing from her. It is my greatest pleasure to take care of Elizabeth, I have loved her since she was born....but this...I cannot countenance it, My Lord!" "Please do not take the will to court, My Dear. That is the only way you could change her bequest to you and what would you tell the judge, Dear....that you do not like money, that you do not honor Madeline's wishes, or what?"

The very quiet Elizabeth, came up and put a hand on her shoulder, "Please are you unhappy…can I help you? Mother told me she was leaving you something and I would not have to worry…but she did not tell me what. Is there a problem, Aunt Ruth?"

"No, Sweetheart, no problem I guess. Just that your dear mother left me much more than I deserve. I am amazed at her generosity!"

"Well, she often said you were the only person she trusted other than Father. She said neither of you liked her for her money as did many others including her relatives and I believed her. You were there for her the whole time she was so ill….the ONLY ONE who gave her peace and help when she needed it so much for a year and I did not know what to do. Please do not be unhappy with her!"

"Oh, my darling girl, I am not unhappy with your mother, just amazed that she, who was so conservative, really frugal and cautious would extend me such wealth. I realize there is still a fortune left for you, but it is amazing to me…simply amazing!"

"Sir Ambrose, please provide me with a name or two of attorneys that I can get to assist me….unless you would like to do so?"

46

"I would indeed, Dear, but I feel I cannot when administering this estate and it is giving substantial money to you. Now I have to continue doing Elizabeth's because Madeline specifically named me to do so and there is no bequest to me….but you should find your own attorney or accountant – I would say attorney because of the size of the bequest. I can recommend a couple to you, who are very dependable, if you would like?"

"Oh, Yes, if you please, Sir. I would be most thankful. My small bequest from my parents is with a bank but this requires more expertise, I believe." Said Ruth.

"If you continue down Madeline's list you will see that she had named anyone who will have authority over her estate and I am honored to be named as such. We will find you someone else. I have a name in mind but will need to get his permission first. I will let you know when you can be introduced to someone. In the meantime, the funds are very secure being in more than one reliable bank and cautiously placed. For today, I wish to continue with your perusal of the will, at least the next three items which are involving Elizabeth."

As she tried to get her breathing calm, she read that he was the primary attorney for Elizabeth with a Lord Justin Albert the secondary and direct consultant for minor questions or distributions to Ruth as financial guardian for Elizabeth, for Ruth's own bequest in this will or for Major Masters' bequest. That anything Elizabeth needed for her happiness, health or education was to be provided after approval and that consideration must be given to advice from Miss Ruth Roberts, aunt of the deceased and guardian for Elizabeth.

"Well, I do not know if I can take in any more today, My Lord. I will gladly take the copies you had made for me and read them with great care. May I make another appointment with you regarding any questions on Elizabeth's estate or mine at that time? I will also be in touch with the person you recommend for me. I see there are some distribution orders here in blank. To use for purchases I make for Elizabeth or the estate, like the piano?"

"Yes, that is correct. Anything you buy that is to be paid for by the estate, except simple petty cash items, should have such a withdrawal slip and then be presented to me for payment….such as a piano, like you mentioned, a new carriage, a large piece of furniture, or for construction of a veranda and so forth. You will find a supply of blank checks for less important items and an authorization form for you to fill in and provide to the bank where the funds are located. As to your distribution, you will decide entirely on those funds and the attorney you choose can recommend a bank of two for your deposit."

"When we left home this morning, I was prepared to make a great appeal for Elizabeth to have a nice pianoforte and lessons, but I guess that would not count now as a big distribution…. I can hardly take it all in! We are on our way now for nuncheon and to purchase such a piano, so you will see a withdrawal for that should we find one we like. Also, to ask about someone to give lessons….I guess now that I see this, it is not a great expense after all." She grinned broadly.

About that time Lord Justin Albert came in and was introduced to both clients. He did an obvious double take upon seeing Ruth Roberts. He smiled broadly and Lord Ambrose realized he was quite taken with how beautiful Ruth Roberts was. He did not say a word, but it was amusing in the extreme because Lord Albert was recognized by staff and many area attorneys as never taking an interest in a female at all and here he was grinning as broadly as an eighteen-year-old!
"Can we invite you to join us for nuncheon Lord Ambrose or Lord Albert?"
"Why I thank you so much but I am expected home for nuncheon today, my wife is entertaining our daughter and her new husband so it is a command performance that I be there. Meanwhile Lord Albert has quite a clientele scheduled while I am away." He said with a big grin.

She and Elizabeth bowed and putting the many papers in her reticule (happy she had brought her larger one), they left for luncheon if she could swallow that is!

Over and over saying to herself how surprised she was, well more than surprised. Overwhelmed! She was a rich woman….how can that be? She had done nothing more but assist her niece as any God-fearing person would have done. And as for helping and befriending Ellie – well, for Heaven's sake who wouldn't? A charming little girl if ever there was one….Oh, Dear, what to do with so much money? A very nice problem to have for sure and certain, but good gracious, well a place at Bath would be more delightful than she had ever dreamed….now breathe, remember to breathe.

Ellie was clinging to her tightly and she realized the child, even with her great understanding, was also flummoxed by the whole proceeding.

CHAPTER FOUR

For nuncheon they mutually agreed on a small tavern with pretty curtains and plants in the window and people that were nicely dressed, going in and out. Elizabeth was very quiet, as she got when nervous, so Aunt Ruth put her arm around her.

"Did you understand most of the conversation with Lord Ambrose?"

"Well, it appears I am very wealthy. Is that right?"

"Yes, Dear, you are indeed. But not to worry about it, okay? We will have good help from Lord Ambrose and Lord Albert or their staff. And of course, discuss things any time you wish. It is not so much a burden as a great advantage. However, as you get older, we will discuss friends and people who may take advantage of you because you are so wealthy. Do not worry a great deal about it now....we will take each thing as it occurs. My only immediate advice is that you not discuss your inheritance with anyone other than me, either attorney, or your Father when he returns."

"Now, we need to calm down, have a good nuncheon since we didn't do much about breakfast. Then of course, we will go down the street and see about a piano."

Entering the tavern, they were greeted warmly by a young lady in a pretty pink apron and a big smile. "Good afternoon, are you ladies here for nuncheon?" "Yes, we certainly are. I hope you have something nice for us today."

After selecting blueberry muffins and fruit salad, Ellie said that was all she wanted. The waitress asked what to drink, and she grinned then and said tea. Ruth could tell she was a bit out of her element but did not interrupt. Ruth ordered ham, cheesed potatoes, current biscuits, the fruit salad and also tea.

Ellie seemed more herself as they ate and started talking about the piano purchase. Ruth explained about various kinds of pianos and thought a small baby grand would be the nicest. She told Ellie not to decide until she saw and heard them and that would give her an idea of what she might like.

The waitress came and asked would they like to try the cheese and egg souffle, just out of the oven and both agreed. The souffle was served along with a couple of slices of brown bread, also warm from the oven so they ate some more.

After paying and leaving extra for a tip, which she explained to Ellie, tips not being exactly normal but a practice Ruth considered correct – an award for good service and not always were wages for the servers very large.

They walked the additional block to the piano store. It was in a very large building and there were eight pianos on display. A Mr. Thomas Pierce introduced himself and encouraged them to look over the instruments. Four small uprights and three grands....one very large and two about the size Ruth had thought would be right for them but did not say a word while Ellie listened to the man explain each to her and let her touch the keys for the sound quality. While out of her element, she still was using her intellect to notice the difference in tone, appearance, and size.

Aunt Ruth told her she did not have to pick one today, if she was not certain or did not like any but if the opposite and she had found one she really did like for its sound, then they would give the owner a payment order to be sent to her attorney to be paid.

With the encouragement of the salesman, who was most patient and cooperative, Ellie picked the very one that Ruth thought was the best. They explained where it was to be delivered and that they had a draft provided by Lord Edward Ambrose that she, as guardian must sign off on and it would be paid upon presentation to his office in the next block. There was much bowing and nodding of heads.

She inquired when they would deliver it so that staff would be prepared for its placement and they replied in two days – Wednesday. Ruth said they had the room ready, with furniture rearranged and the delivery people should come to the back of the house – over part of the lawn, but that would be acceptable. When they saw the big glass conservatory doors, that is where the piano would be unloaded. Before parting she gave succinct directions to the estate.

He explained that they would provide a considerable number of pieces of sheet music for her, included in the price both hymns and concert pieces, that the bench with a lid to open and store the music was also being delivered and a tuner would come at delivery to be certain nothing had changed in the move.

Ruth asked could they provide the name and contact information for an instructor, and a sheet of paper with that on it was provided showing three listings. They said a favorite teacher for new students would be given the address to stop by as well. All seemed exactly correct and Ruth issued the first draft she would make on Ellie's account.

Horace was waiting outside the piano store and Ellie immediately asked him if he had eaten nuncheon. He grinned broadly at her and said he had indeed including a pint of ale. He had eaten a meat pie and apple compote – two of his favorite things.

Ellie got in the carriage, telling him they had bought a piano, an actual piano with bench and all. He winked at Ruth and told Ellie he looked forward to hearing her play. She laughed and said much as she had to staff that he may not enjoy it for a while until she learned how to play properly. He climbed up onto the seat for driving. Ruth asked that while she was in London, please take her by her bank and giving him directions. She took Elizabeth in with her to acquaint the child with what a bank looked like and how to withdraw money. The child looked askance at the huge safe, the uniformed and armed guards and the bars in front of the clerks. But Ruth explained it was to prevent robberies and not to keep them out. After receiving her money, they went back out to the carriage and Horace drove them toward home. Ellie was enthralled with the many things they passed. More shops showing what they sold by display in the windows, one with pretty dresses, including shawls. She asked if she could buy a new dress sometime and Ruth assured her they would make a shopping trip for such very soon. If they did not find one just right, they would look at yard goods and pick something pretty and yards of trimmings. Ruth knew a seamstress who was really good and would come to the house and measure Ellie so the dress would fit the way she wanted.

On the way home on a different street than they had used that morning, Ellie got excited when she saw two urns at a house that were very elegant. They contained draping ivy, variegated greenery, deep purple flowers in a circle and in the middle a few tall plants with pink blossoms all along the stems. "Oh, look, Aunt Ruth, just look. That has to be the very prettiest one yet!" Ruth agreed mentioning the pink were gladiolas and mentally made note of the street and house number to let Henry know what Ellie had liked.

By the time they got home from their big adventure, Ellie was asleep on Ruth's lap. Horace opened the door and gently took her in his arms. As they got to the house James had it open and Horace took Ellie upstairs and placed her carefully on her bed. Ruth heard a soft mewing coming from the closet, so after taking Ellie's shoes off and placing a light cover over the child, she went to the closet and picked up the little kitten to take him to the yard. Amazingly it looked like he had not used the dirt box, so it was ascertain he needed to go outside.

With the kitten, her arithmetic and reading, as well as horseback riding, Ellie kept busy on Tuesday. On Wednesday she took the kitten outside a while but was so enthusiastic about the arrival of the pianoforte that she could not stand to go to the barn and miss a minute of the excitement, eventually taking Jimbo upstairs to his closet. So, she and Ruth worked on her lessons, including arithmetic, in order to make the time go faster.

Before nuncheon there was the rattle of a huge wagon pulled by four large draft horses and with a tarpaulin over everything. Coming, as instructed to the back of the house, and drawing up closely to the big doors of the study – now to be the conservatory. The men seemed pleased that furniture had been moved out of the way. The butler, Robert, a man of large strong build, rushed to open the study doors as wide as they would go and fasten them with the curved brass fixtures attached to the walls. Then moving to the wagon, he offered his assistance to move the piano inside.

Two of the four men, who had arrived on the wagon, began folding up the coverlet and removing blocks under the rollers on the piano, while the other two removed the top portion, which to Ellie looked like a lid, and as the butler rushed to help them, carried it separately into the room, resting it carefully against the bookcase. Ellie noticed that the piano was on rollers, what a good idea, so much easier to move, she had no idea how it could be lifted even with so many men and those from the house as well. It looked even bigger than it had in the music store.

Then the five men secured a long ramp with metal clips to the wagon bed on the side closest to the study doors. They began to slowly ease the giant piano off the wagon and down the ramp, having great effort to keep it from rolling down too fast. Finally, successfully getting it into the room. Ellie was amazed that it had happened without accident! She then realized she was clutching Aunt Ruth's hand so

tightly it was getting blue. Aunt Ruth laughed and
said it was quite all right, a very exciting time and
such skilled workers to get the large thing off the
wagon and into the room with little difficulty.

A couple quilted blankets were taken off of many
wires under the lid of the piano – protection for the
workings of the instrument as it was transported. The
top of the piano was reattached, the music rack
unloaded from the wagon and also fastened, then the
bench unwrapped from its blanket and carried inside
as well.

One gentleman, obviously the spokesman, came
forward and handed Ellie a large pile of what looked
like music books and sheet music. Ascertaining the
piano sounded as it should, one of the organ men
began playing many cords and a few quick tunes to
be certain the move had not created any problems.
Ellie, not being knowledgeable of music, decided he
must know how to play because it was very nice. She
so hoped at some time in the future she would be able
to play just as he had.

The man came up to Aunt Ruth and gave her a paper
with a name and address of the lady they
recommended to teach Ellie. He stated they were
familiar with her and that she was neat and pleasant
but the best thing about her was that she could play
and teach very well and specialized in teaching
people who did not currently know how to play a
piano. He felt certain the Miss would be pleased with

58

her but in the pile of music was a list of three other teachers besides the ones given to them Monday, should they need them. Bowing they left after carefully folding up the ramp on the wagon, taking the stocks from under the wheels that held it steady, and also getting the horses to move.

Ellie stood and looked at her long wished-for piano and realized she was speechless. How would she ever, ever be able to play such a grand and elegant thing! She had heard how beautiful it was when the gentlemen tested it but could she ever do such? Oh my, well she would try, but she had doubts.

She was encouraged by Aunt Ruth, the rest of that afternoon, to just play with the keys, tinkling as she wished and getting used to the varying sounds of both the black and white ones. She enjoyed that more than she had thought and made up "noises," as she called them. She did like that the sounds at one end were deep and at the other were higher. She made up ideas of her own mixing the white and black notes...no idea what they were but enjoying the experiment. Laughing when the sounds were not in accord.

Later she and Aunt Ruth enjoyed their dinner while discussing music lessons, the cat, horse-back riding, and the start of school very soon. Well, life was certainly interesting lately. She fell asleep early with thoughts of piano keys and kitten purrs in her head.

Ellie had hoped to ride her horse the next day, Thursday, but it was raining. Having eaten breakfast and played with the kitten, she agreed with Aunt Ruth to examine her wardrobe as to what fit, what she had outgrown, any mending needed and things she really did not want to wear anymore. She had a good many dresses in her closet but after removing several, she realized she did not have a plenty left. Her dark blue one that she had worn to Mother's funeral was in the back of the closet and Aunt Ruth said she need not wear it again now but they would keep it there. Her very favorite was a light blue with lace and two petticoats attached underneath. She told Aunt Ruth that she thought of it as her Sunday dress, usually wearing it only to church.

Making notes as to colors and ideas Ellie had for new dresses, Aunt Ruth said they would call a dressmaker to come and measure and if possible bring samples of material from which she could choose what she would like. Well, now, how about that – she would choose? Things certainly were different around here. Just as they were finishing and rehanging the dresses still wearable, Janie tapped on the door and said the piano teacher had arrived.

Ellie was ecstatic! She had no idea Aunt Ruth had already sent a note to the piano teacher. She bolted from the room and sped downstairs. Aunt Ruth was only a short distance behind her.

In the hall stood a tall, slim woman, well really just a girl, who was smiling and asked if she was the person needing piano lessons? Ellie nodded emphatically, then remembering her manners said: "Oh, yes Ma'am, I am indeed. Is she my teacher, Aunt Ruth?" "Well, yes, if she is Mistress Ann West. How do you do, Miss West. As you can see Ellie is quite excited to learn to play the piano and very happy you could come so quickly."
"There is no need for formality, I find it is easiest if we are just on a first name basis, if you don't mind that is?"
"Oh, I don't mind at all…Ann, please call me Ellie."
"Two of my students, a brother and sister, have left for boarding school and your invitation to teach here came at an opportune time. It will be easy to work you in two days a week, if that is satisfactory. Thursday and Monday would be convenient but I can make it different days if those do not suit, Ma'am" She said looking at Ruth.
"We are pleased with Thursdays and Mondays in the afternoon after school. Should anything else interrupt, we will let you know. Just leave me your address for contact. Please call me Ruth. This is a very excited Ellie and the piano was delivered yesterday. They assure me it is in tune and ready to

be played. Would you like to come through to the music room and try it out?"

"Oh, yes, I had hoped it was delivered, being anxious to see it. Mr. Pence told me which one you had picked and it is indeed a fine instrument. I have given lessons at their establishment and am quite familiar with the pianos they currently have. This one would have been my pick as well."

Ellie took the girl's hand and led her to the study – now music room. "Ma'am, can you play something for me? So, I can hear how it should sound when I have worked hard to learn."

"Oh, yes I would be glad to play for you. I will start with something simple so you can see that in the beginning it will not be so terribly difficult."

Ruth was so pleased to see Ellie's rapt attention as the young lady began to play a well-known tune but without extra keys and embellishments.

As she finished, Ellie clapped her small hands. Ann smiled and said it was her turn, she would show her how to play a scale first and not to mind if she hit a wrong key or forgot which ones – that was to be expected with a new student and she would learn the correct way after some lessons.

Ellie looked alarmed but scooted more toward the middle of the bench as directed and the teacher stood behind her and showed her which keys to press. Ellie followed directions exactly and after three tries could duplicate the little trill of notes on her own. She looked over at Aunt Ruth with a big smile.

Ruth told them she had things to do and would return in a little while. Knowing if she was there it might take Ellie's attention away from the task at hand.

As she left the room, she heard Ellie again play the scale with only one mistake and then redo it exactly right. Well, she knew the child was bright but was amazed at how quickly she had understood that first little lesson. The next half hour was not always that successful but not terribly trying on the ears either.

Overall, it was quite good. Before she left, the teacher showed Ellie on a strip of music she provided which written note compared to which key she had been hitting and had her play it again four times. Then she withdrew from her reticule two additional strips of notes for Ellie to figure out before her next lesson.

Ellie had never been so happy. Of course, she missed her Mother and cried about her on occasion, but she was busy enough that she did not mope or seem terribly distraught. Ruth thought it had to be some relief to the child to not see her mother in such terrible pain and wasting away.

Ellie thought of her father often, too. Wondering where he was in the world, what war had called him this time. Her mother would get regular letters and read them and kept them all in her dresser.

Sometimes Ellie would get a letter from him too. But she had not heard from him in forever, since well before her Mother died. What was that about? Why did he not come when Mother needed him so badly and called for him as she got worse and worse?

She cried sometimes but it did no good – it had not saved her Mother and had not brought her Father home.

Trying to get herself cheerful again, she realized she was the busiest ever. Busiest of her whole life. She took care of Jimbo. She rode the horse everyday if there was no rain, thanking Big Jim profusely after each ride. Sometimes she was accompanied by Aunt Ruth on a horse as well. She even put tack away and curried the horses. She attended her school for about five hours each weekday. She read stories to Aunt Ruth to perfect her reading and word sounding. She even did arithmetic when insisted upon by Aunt Ruth. She really did NOT like arithmetic.

She didn't forget to talk with Henry about the potted plants to have placed beside the front door, asking Aunt Ruth to tell him the address of the ones she had liked best.

Of course, she practiced her piano at least three or four times a day. Helped organize her closet, hanging two new dresses Aunt Ruth had sent for. And continued to carry her dirty dishes to the kitchen for staff.

Ellie was doing hard thinking on Sunday night. She decided she needed to go to the cemetery and talk to her Mother. Aunt Ruth accompanied her. She was crying softly and knelt beside the grave. "Dear Mama, I miss you so much! Please do not mind that I have been happy with Aunt Ruth. I love you Mama! When I play the piano, I hope you can hear me in Heaven. Mama, I try to be a good girl as you would wish. I love you Mama." Crying she stood up and ran to the house. Well, tarnation Ruth was crying too! When staff brought in dinner, Ruth noticed that Janice had red eyes and thought the kitchen staff must know about the visit to the cemetery. Well, that was all right, they would appreciate that the child had not forgotten the woman who loved Ellie but was so harshly raised that she had trouble expressing it.

The piano lesson on Monday went exceedingly well. All the practice Ellie had put in paid off with compliments and looks toward Ruth of surprise. Ellie admitted she had trouble with the one paper and the teacher was able to show her how to better reach the correct keys and had her replay it several times, most of which were correct.
They played two little tunes Ellie had heard before and she was really happy to be able to almost duplicate them flawlessly after considerable practice. Ruth knew she would hear them the next few days,

realizing Ellie would work hard to have them error free by the next lesson on Thursday.

Later that afternoon Ellie had a surprise. Henry came to the barn to find her just as she finished riding with Big Jim. She was now confident enough, in just the short while, to sit upon the horse without Jim holding the back of her dress. She was making progress in all things it seemed and happier by the day.

When she saw Henry approaching, she wondered if he had seen the flower arrangements at the house in town. Henry asked her, if she was finished with her horse, could she please come to the front porch and help him. Hoping it was something to do with the flowers, like where to place them when they came, she nodded but stated she had to put her tack away and curry the horse first. Big Jim came up and stated if she put the tack away properly he would curry her horse for her this time. So, grinning, it was arranged and she did not see Jim wink at Henry.

Following Henry into the house and through to the front door, Ellie saw Ruth there first and then realized the whole porch looked covered with all kinds of things. Two huge iron planters on nice tall bases, two big baskets full of a rich, dark dirt, two long boxes with lovely pink flowers growing along tall stems, another box with ivy and plants with purple flowers, and two big bushy white flowered plants in burlap sacks.

"I hope you don't mind, Miss, but I thought you might like yours a little different and so I got the biggest urns and the white flowers to go in the center front of each. Is that all right? If not, we can plant the white ones at the end of the walkway near the drive, Miss, whichever suits."

She rushed up and hugged him, totally alarming the old man. "Oh, you are so wonderful to do this so quickly. The flowers you picked are so beautiful and I am certain will look exactly right. Can we plant them now....I will help you!"

Ruth, complete with a large apron over her skirt, announced she would provide an extra pair of hands. Together the three worked for over an hour. Henry putting some of the rich soil into each big pot, then showing the "girls" how the tall plants went in next, trying to have them stand up straight by adding soil around their stems. Following that, the ivy draped over the edges with the roots carefully covered with some soil, Henry explaining the purple flowers would help hold the ivy in place as well and that the ivy would multiply until it was a heartier drape. They added the purple, leaving a space in the front for the bunches of white blooms and finishing the whole thing off with a generous amount of the rich dark soil. Then Ellie noticed he had big pots with water and they gave each urn a generous drink., pouring in a circle around the plants to wet each one's roots.

Standing back, tired, and dirty, Ellie was grinning as broadly as her mouth would widen. "Oh, Henry, I thank you so much. They are beautiful! Just exactly the way I had hoped. Thank you, thank you."

Pointing to the one on the left, she said: "This one is Mother's" and then pointing to the other one, "This one is Father's." Henry had to turn away, after all a grown man couldn't let a small child see him cry! While Ruth did not even hide her tears. Ellie ran into the house calling for everyone to come to the porch. Looking askance, most staff who were not stirring pots in the kitchen came and everyone marveled at their spectacular front porch. Wasn't it lovely seeing Miss Ellie enjoying something!

As he collected himself, Henry explained they would need water every day and should he forget or be away, then Ellie should see that staff did not forget to water them when needed. Being on the porch they would not get the benefit of any rain and so would need tending in order to not wilt and die. Ellie solemnly nodded that she understood.

As they cleaned up for dinner, including an early bath and different clothes, Ellie asked Aunt Ruth if Henry had any family. Ruth said she was not aware of any but was not certain. She knew he had been at this estate since before Ellie was born and never with a wife but she knew little about him. Ellie nodded solemnly. "That is too bad, everyone needs someone to love them. Big Jim has his Annie, and Julie has Edward, and I have you, wouldn't it be nice if Henry had someone too?"

"Well, child that is something we cannot pick out for him. Should he find someone on his own, we can certainly congratulate him, but I don't believe he would appreciate our interference."

"Oh, all right. I just wondered." Said a serious Ellie. After eating a generous portion of everything at dinner, Ellie again went to the front porch to look at her flowers. Going down the steps and walking to the road, she turned and looked at her house. Oh, very nice! It looked more like a home now. She carefully studied the place. To her it looked like a castle. The corners each had big square stone columns and turrets and the windows had curved stone tops with heavy stone sills. Very well constructed she imagined although as a child had never considered such before. Castle-like, however most of the castles in her books had little slits for windows and this house had many big panes of glass in casements. A Glass Castle…that was it! She would call it her Glass Castle! Now if it were a fairy tale, it would have a prince and a princess. Well Aunt Ruth could be the princess; she was not very old and on consideration she was very pretty. Funny she had never thought of

Aunt Ruth as pretty before, but now thinking about it, she was. But unfortunately, there was no prince.

She wondered if Aunt Ruth had ever had a beau? She did not remember her ever bringing either a boy or girl friend to the house. Funny to think of that. Oh, well, she knew it was none of her business, but she could pretend it was a castle and that Aunt Ruth was the princess waiting for her knight. Laughing at herself, she went back in to get ready for bed. She was really tired. She had been busy the entire day. What fun it had been!

As the house quieted, staff thought about the lovely child upstairs and wished so much her father would appear. They were certain this was the longest he had ever been away and it really did not bode well. He appeared to love his wife, Ellie's mother, very dearly. They did not think he would take another woman friend but what in the world had kept him away so long? True he was military through and through but certainly he would have deserved leave by now. Of course, the war with France had been long and awful. They wondered if he knew what he was missing in having so very lovely a daughter and she was incredibly smart and caring. Their prayers were for the child but also the father.

Just before Ellie went to sleep it dawned on her that she would turn nine in just four weeks. She wondered if anyone would remember. Aunt Ruth might not. She did not have a party last year, because Mother had started to get sick. This year Mother was not here to remind anyone and she had no idea if staff paid attention to anything like that or not.

Oh well, it made no difference, she had so many wonderful things. She got to ride, pet her kitten, she had lots of books, she had just gotten two new dresses and best of all the piano with lessons too! See, it did not matter about her birthday….she was getting nice things every day, like weeks of one big celebration. And she certainly did not need any flowers…her whole porch was beautiful with flowers. On that happy note her tired body finally went to dreams.

The past two weeks had been exhausting and Ruth realized on this Tuesday morning she had not slept all that well either. Her mind kept going to Major Masters and his mysterious disappearance. How she wished he would show up for Ellie. The child was doing really well, with so many distractions like piano, kitten, horse, school, extra reading and flowers, but parents are important to a child, what in tarnation had kept him away all this time? The one thing possible that he could not have changed was something she could not bear to think of…might he have been killed or injured on the battlefield? For Ellie to lose both parents would be awful beyond any nightmare. She would try not to think of that as the issue, but it seemed the only solution to his being missing so long.

Hearing a gentle tap at her door, she realized she had been daydreaming and was not finished dressing. Opening the door to Ellie, the child looked at her and then laughed. Laughed of all things!

"Well, Missy, I am glad I amuse you…come in here and help me finish dressing so we can eat and you can practice your piano." They both laughed as intended, Ellie did her buttons in back and they headed downstairs for a hearty breakfast. The sun was out nicely so after music they could ride a while.

CHAPTER FIVE

Unbeknownst to them it was going to be a difficult Tuesday evening but so far the day progressed well, music played, horses ridden, flowers watered, book read, and nuncheon eaten, even a small amount of arithmetic completed; for school was upon them and Ruth wanted Ellie to be a good student. While she missed some sleep last night, Ruth had made up a few samples of arithmetic problems for Ellie to do and while Ruth read a book, the child sat at the desk and did the arithmetic. Ellie was not fond of such, but it did no good to complain, knowing it was necessary and that Aunt Ruth would be pleased if she did them well.

Just past noon mealtime there was the rattle of a large carriage or wagon on the gravel beside the house, loud enough it was heard throughout. The butler, Robert, hurried to the door, opening it to a very large man in a military uniform. He inquired if Lady Madeline Aker Masters, wife of Major Alfred Troy Masters was available. Robert answered that he regretted to report that Lady Masters had passed away, how may he be of help?"
The officer looked at him askance. "Oh, please tell me that is not so. We have come so far and he cannot be returned for he will surely die."

"I beg your pardon, officer, but I do not know what you are talking about. Lady Masters was buried two weeks ago in the cemetery on this very property. Please explain why you needed to see her!" He heard Ruth, who was standing behind him, gasp and sob.

Ruth stepped forward and inquired: "Who would die and who is in the large wagon, pardon, Lieutenant?"

"Excuse me, Ma'am, but Major Alfred Troy Masters is in the wagon. He is in dire health from multiple wounds and only recently could be moved. He is alive but barely and I am most certain he cannot live to travel much further – if he survives through the night at all!"

"Lieutenant, this is the correct address, his home. We had no idea where he was or that he was coming to us. We have had no correspondence in some time."

"We transported him as soon as possible. He has spoken so fondly of his wife and daughter, we brought him as soon as he could be moved! He has been fully awake only a few of days, but the trip has him unconscious again. I regret, but I am not certain of his chances of recovery."

"Oh, Sir, I am his daughter's aunt. You may call me Ruth." She turned quickly and said: "Henry, hurry and send help to the room that Lady Masters used. Notify staff we will need all medicines and bandages gathered, extra bedding – as much as possible - and have the bed turned back and warmed immediately!"

Henry ran in the direction of the kitchen to gather all staff he could.

Turning back to the officer, Ruth said: "Continue around the house and I will meet you at the large green back door. There are no steps and it will be easier for you to transport him. Then please bring him right in, I will direct you.. Be prepared to explain his injuries to me as soon as we can get him settled." Ruth looked behind her and said, "Janie, turn back the bed and open the door wide to the room Lady Masters used. Light lamps, too please. Bring a bed warmer, warm water, warm herbal tea with plenty of sugar, a bottle of rum, and all salves and medicines of which you can think. Have staff bring the box of bandages left from Lady Masters that are in the cupboard in my dressing room. Send someone from the kitchen to get Jim from the stables and then have him light a fire."

She noticed Ellie, standing there, and sobbing but not saying a word. "Come, Sweetheart, you will help me, please. It appears your father had not come home earlier because of his injuries.. You will help me nurse him. Here I will unbutton you, now run and put on an older dress and then bring the roll of bandages in the green box in my chest, plus the blue cover at the foot of my bed. I will button you if you don't see any staff to do so. Hurry, Love." Given a job to do, made Ellie take a deep breath and hurry away, as

Ruth had intended. Poor child, first her mother, hardly cold yet, and now her father also dying…well, maybe not. They would make every effort to get him better!

Ellie was back almost immediately; she must have run very fast. Ruth buttoned her and then said: "Good girl! Now find all the extra bed pillows you can and bring them to your mother's old sick room. If you can carry an extra blanket that too, if not go back for one. Thank you, Darling!" She had Janie line up the supplies on the dresser in the sick room, while she hurried to the back door. She heard the large wagon being stopped with a loud "Halt" to the horses. She had the door wide open and thankfully the sun was just past high, so there was sufficient light. Four men, two in uniform were carrying a cot with the unconscious Major Alfred Troy Masters. He was tall, and although ill, carried some weight and the men helping were having a time negotiating the hallway but they managed to get him into the room. Other staff had successfully turned back the bed, lit the lamps, and were placing all manner of medicines, a tea pot, rum, the medicine-spout pitcher, and towels on the dresser. Hurriedly removing the bed warmer. They had placed extra bedding on the couch and Ellie was adding some more to that pile. Thomas had brought a slop jug, wash basin, bucket of hot water and from his pockets took out soap and a dozen washing rags. Ruth quickly asked them to put some older extra bedding down for underneath him since he was unconscious and might mess up the bed frequently – they needed to protect the mattress if possible. Ruth continued giving other orders as she felt necessary and noticed one of the military men grinning. "May I help you, Sir?" "Oh, I beg your pardon Ma'am, but I appreciate the way you are organizing things – you would have been a nice addition to the military!"

"We have some of his paperwork here, where shall we put it that it doesn't get wet?" Said another in a tired looking uniform and worried expression.

"Oh, here I will take it and put it in this drawer. Just call me Ruth."

"Thank you so much for helping him, he has lain in a hospital for some weeks unconscious off and on - but is still very gravely ill. The military doctors are limited in supplies and expertise, so we hope that bringing him home will get him better. He distinguished himself beyond imagination and we would wish him to spend any time left with his wife and daughter. He has talked so fondly of them since he awoke!" We will do everything possible to help the Major get well, Lieutenant."

Ruth walked the Army men out to their wagon, asking what had happened to Major Masters. They stated he had single-handedly held off the surge of over one hundred opposing Frenchmen, protecting six officers and twenty infantry, all severely wounded for thirteen days although very injured himself! He will be awarded several medals in the near future. He had regained full consciousness just recently after weeks of lethargy. He will be distressed about his right arm, but gangrene had set in and the doctors at the hospital had to remove it to save his life. They were so sorry for him and pray he will get better now he is home.

She thanked them for bringing him back. She bid them God speed and went back inside.

Henry and Thomas were assisting her and groaned as they saw his condition. As the army blanket was removed from Major Masters by Robert, Ruth gasped. Ellie's father, looking emaciated, was bandaged almost from head to foot. And horrors, a portion of his right arm was missing from just below the shoulder! That was what the military man had meant. Some of the bandages were bloody and most were very dirty. This would NOT do!

He groaned, which at least showed him to be alive for his breathing was so sallow, it was hard to see if he really was breathing at all. Ruth wet a clean and soft wash rag with warm water and a little soap and began washing his face and neck. He groaned but did not seem as if he didn't want it done, just as recognition that someone had touched him. While still a tall man he was a fraction of his former self.

Ribs prominent, cheeks sunken in, and hip bones looking like they would pierce the skin! He looked awful! How would she ever keep him alive and help him get better? Well, not on her watch would he die! She put a spoon of warm, sweet tea on his lips and at first there was no indication he knew. She wiped it away and did it again and again until he licked it off. Still appearing unconscious but at least part of him moved! The only parts of his body that were currently visible and not bandaged were his nose, lips, one eye, left hand, part of his right thigh, and his feet.

This room was large enough for people to get on either side of the bed to comfort or wash the patient, so it was the correct room for Major Masters. After successfully getting one half a cup of sweet tea into him a spoonful at a time, Ruth began to wash him with warm soapy water. Finishing his face, ears, and neck, plus a little of his chest that wasn't one giant dirty bandage. She then washed his remaining hand, which was unbandaged and the parts of the other upper arm and shoulder that stuck out of another filthy wrapping.

She next fixed the medicine spouted cup full of tea adding generous sugar and a few dollops of rum. She was again successful getting him to swallow that as she tipped it into his mouth a little bit at a time, while her other hand could hold his head up enough so he didn't choke. She had asked Thomas to bring Big Jim from the stables and for them to assist her by raising him as gently as possible so she could wash him a little more and examine his shoulders, and back. She cut away the very dirty shirt and threw it into a trash basket. There was a nasty cut and abrasion on his right shoulder but it was virtually healed, so she just washed it well with good soapy water and applied salve. The rest of his back, that she could see, was scraped and unpleasantly covered with rash. She washed it well, added a little salve and then carefully laid a clean folded sheet under his upper body parts that she had attended. As they laid him back down, he sighed a pleasant sound so evidently they hadn't hurt him with the movement and washing.

"Here, Ellie, bring me another clean rag that is wet with warm water and soapy. This rag needs to be thrown out. Then please go to the kitchen and ask for a pail to collect the dirty rags for I already have the waste can full. Ask staff to hunt up every wash rag they can find including tearing up a couple of the older sheets to make more!" Ellie thought as she ran to the kitchen: "What kind of black cloud had descended on this house! First her dear Mother, so very ill for so long and now her big, strong father looking like he might not live until morning. What kind of punishment was this? Where was God? Did he not care about them at all? In what condition was he…would he live until tomorrow, next week, another year?" She got the bucket and some clean rags staff provided and crying, rushed back to the room. She didn't know much about nursing but was learning for sure and certain, first her Mother's illness and now, well now she obviously would learn more. He was so injured! Ellie had wondered where her father was, the continent, a hospital, dead, abroad in another direction like the islands, fighting in the Americas. It had been a puzzlement and here he had indeed been so injured! Balderdash!

Ellie put a footstool up to the far side of the bed, stepping up, and using a clean wet cloth rubbed with soap, began to wash his hand and the part of his left arm and chest not bandaged. She then got another, likewise, wetting and soaping it and going to the other bedside, removed a loose and dirty bandage and washed his lower leg, which was scabbed and bruised but not bleeding and no open wounds. She looked up and Ruth was smiling at her to indicate it was the correct thing to do. Next she washed both his feet, while Ruth was again spooning tea into him and when not doing that Ruth was washing his neck, chest and the part of his shoulder not bandaged. She took a blanket and heated it by holding it in front of the fire that Thomas had lit. She placed it over his chest and he sighed. Ellie had taken the salve and was applying it to the areas she had washed that had abrasions, as she had seen Ruth do.

About that time Big Jim whispered to Ruth that he would undress the Major completely so he could be washed everywhere else. He would then have clean bedding put down as he held him up. He would also use clean bandages and remove any old that were not sticking to wounds. Thomas said he would help and while the two big sturdy men did that she and Ellie could go to the kitchen for a bite to eat. Ruth had not realized how long they had been attending the Major but it was now dark outside and she should be certain Ellie had repast. Robert came back in with more bedding. Well good! With three strong men, it should make quick work of washing the patient and changing his bedding. She would tell the staff that an early washing of bedding would be needed in the morning, for it was a dirty and bloody job they faced and would take many sheets and blankets.

Ruth and Ellie washed their hands and arms thoroughly with soap and pitchers of warm water provided by staff. Then they went and asked the kitchen help for their supper.. Both nodded that roasted chicken sounded good and they took their seats. After eating quickly, they returned to the sick room. Ellie having refused to go up to bed. Ruth did not insist. The child had lost one parent recently, let her stay and help the other one, she could sleep later. Big Jim said they had no knowledge if the Major had left any clothes here and Ruth went to check. She felt the Major's room, was the bedroom adjoining Madeline's room upstairs, she and Ellie found it was and in the dresser were underthings, shirts, and stockings. Plus, they stripped the bed of sheets and two blankets. Each taking an armload, they hurried downstairs. She tapped on the door and when told to enter brought forth her pile of gentlemen's wearing apparel and bedding. Big Jim grinned and said, "Just in time. Excuse us ladies we have finished the bathing and will dress him in clean undershirt right away. No pants because he is incontinent. We will call you when ready.

Waiting in the hall seemed forever, sitting forlornly on two side chairs, hoping the bathing and fresh clothes would feel good to the Major – if he could feel that is! Ruth was mentally organizing a refreshing of bandages for any areas the men did not do and wondering what nourishment she should provide. She decided chicken broth, and more tea were the best at this stage. Doris came down the hall to inquire if any special nourishment was needed. Ruth explained that a rich chicken broth would be nourishing but easily digested. She said, of course more sweet tea. She would add rum every once in a while too. She asked Doris to find an upstairs maid

83

and inquire if there was any additional salves in the house. Please have them brought to the sick room. Thanking Doris, she hugged Ellie and they sat and waited. She dreaded the smell of camphor from the salve but knew it was the best for open wounds with not much else being available. She looked at the pile of extremely dirty and bloody rags or old clothes in a pail outside the door and instructed a staff person to see they were burned Although it seemed a long time, Ruth was certain it had not been, when Robert and Thomas exited the bedroom, looking wet and tired. "We have done as good a job of cleaning him up as possible at this time. He is weary and we do not want to bother him too much more tonight. Big Jim said he will stay the whole night. While you were having dinner, Jamison Pike came by to inquire and I took the liberty of sending him by horse and with a lantern for the doctor. He should be back shortly with or without the physician's attendance."

"Oh, thank you so much Robert! Let's hope that Jamison finds the doctor available. We will prevail, regardless, but it would be good to know what a professional thinks!"

She cleared the settee of the extra bedding and things – putting them on the pile on the floor and then indicated Big Jim could use the settee to rest. They would stay on chairs until too tired and go to their bedrooms once certain it looked like the Major would survive the night, she told Ellie.

CHAPTER SIX

On occasion the Major would groan or try to move but was too weak to make any substantial change in his position. Ellie occasionally would go and whisper to him and smooth his hair or gently touch his face, it was more than Ruth or Jim could stand to see. Ruth was about ready to insist Ellie go to bed when James came in with Doctor Ormand. He took one look at the Major and shook his head, which he realized too late made Ellie cry. "It is all right Little One, I am just distressed at his condition as I am certain are you. Here I will examine him. He is obviously alive and so we have that in our favor." Big Jim helped the doctor lift the covers off the Major's chest and the doctor used his ear trumpet to listen to the breathing and heart rate. "Well, good news, there is congestion but I don't believe it is full blown pneumonia. His heart is beating a little slowly but not more than one would expect from his condition and better than too fast. See here, I have brought some medicine to give him when you are certain he is swallowing properly – it won't do for it to go into his lungs. This is to be used in place of any alcohol, such as the rum you have given him. Two hours after each eight-hour dose, you may again use the tea and rum mixture. Give him all the plain tea, lemonade or water he will take any time. If he is able in the morning, give him strong chicken broth – not too much salt in it. All he will take and of course continue with the tea and rum. I will return tomorrow evening."

"Thank you so much, Dr. Ormand! We appreciate your attendance on the Major so late in the evening. We shall expect you tomorrow. We will have people with him all night and make him as comfortable as possible. We have bathed him completely, with the help of three of our men. His body was in terrible condition, rashes as you have seen, dirty beyond words, and so many injuries that I am most afraid of infection. We will be vigilant, Sir."
"Oh, Miss Roberts, you have done tremendously! It is a credit to you that he is as restful as he is and a wonder to you all that he is now clean and I am certain more comfortable as a result. Keep up the good works…he will need great care, but I know how wonderfully you took care of Lady Masters and trust he will be well cared for. Good Evening."
Finally, Ruth took Ellie up to bed, telling her she would be needed on the morrow to help with her Father so must get some sleep now. That seemed to work and the exhausted child crawled under the covers, several hours past her normal bedtime.
Ruth made a mental note to let the butler know to contact the piano teacher that they would have to postpone lessons for a while but she would be paid.

Ruth looked wishfully down the hall toward her room. Deciding she would just get a sweater, but not stay even though Jim had suggest she sleep a while. Sweater in hand and another bunch of gauze bandages from the cabinet in her washroom, she reappeared in the sick room. Jim grinned at her – "Just couldn't stay away?" She shook her head "no." About that time, the Major gave a mighty effort and tried to sit up. His eyes were closed, so they did not know if he was asleep and doing it or conscious. Jim immediately went to the bedside to prevent him falling out of it and Ruth hurried to the other, wiping his brow with warm, wet cloths. Between the two of them, they heard him sigh and give up on whatever attempt he was making. They wondered if he had any idea where he was or if he was still fighting a battle in his mind. Jim placed extra towels under his lower body again to absorb any urine or perspiration that was expelled.

Several times during the night one or the other of them would give him tea or broth and wipe his brow or straighten his covers. He did not thrash around much but was starting to move his legs and being such a very tall man although terribly thin, even the double sized bed was small for him. Neither Jim nor Ruth got any sleep, worrying that he would try to get up since he had moved again like the first time. All night they attended him. By daylight they both looked hollow-eyed and exhausted.

Janie had come in to check on them and said she was getting the kitchen girls to fix them a breakfast tray with fresh hot tea, scones, and scrambled eggs. Ruth asked that they do an eggnog for the patient too – making it thin but tasty and they could see if he would take it. A good idea although not prescribed by the doctor and she and Jim both said in unison to ask staff to bring fresh hot water. As she left Janie said Ellie was sleeping well.

Ruth still had a good bit of salve to use on the cuts that had been rubbed by the bedding and aggravated by his transport in the wagon. Jim reached under the covers periodically and again put a wad of old towels under the patient since he would obviously not be getting up to use a waste chair but with all the tea and medicine it would save the bedding.

As light from the windows increased with dawn, they both turned as they heard the door open, thinking Janie had returned with a question or something and there was a sleepy Elizabeth, she had dressed herself but needed buttoning and forgotten to comb her hair but her main concern was looking about her father. After assurance he had spent a good night considering all his damages, she seemed very relieved. Ruth braided her hair and tied it off with strips of rags. Madeline would be furious.

When breakfast arrived, Ruth insisted the kitchen did not need to do anything for Elizabeth but that they would share the generous plate of food. After eating all they could, Ruth started trying to get the Major to take nourishment. Finally succeeding in getting almost a cup of tea into him and a little of the egg yolk diluted with tea. Next it was time for his medicine left by Dr. Ormond. That was a little more difficult because he did not want to cooperate. Well, that was good...it showed he was starting to make decisions and awaken. With several attempts she did get him to down his medicine and enough water too. The next visitor was Robert, who insisted Jim go home and get a few hours rest. The barn animals had been taken care of by Williams and nothing needed to be done but for Jim to sleep. Upon insistence from Ruth, he left promising to return after a nap. Janie asked Robert to bring in the big, padded rocking chair from the library and she would just rest that way but since the Major may be waking, she would not want to leave the room. She told Ellie to be her lookout and if the Major began to wake up, let her know if she was asleep.

She was very, very tired but really not sleepy – being too disturbed by the patient's illness to relax enough to actually sleep. Ellie scooted out and got one of her schoolbooks and brought it back to read, while hoping that Father would wake up and speak. Time seemed to drag. On the occasion that the patient moaned or seemed to be able to listen to her, Ruth would try to wake him enough to get broth or custard into him. He was nothing but skin and bones! Jim had changed the pile of towels catching any waste again, and she asked staff to bring more clean rags. At least his body was working. Now hopefully, his mind would at some time too. She was getting his medicine to go down at the appointed time for each dose – Dr. Ormond would be pleased!

The Major, Alfred Troy Masters, was awake but didn't want to indicate that. He was trying first to figure out where he could possibly be…he definitely wasn't in a field hospital. No field hospital had a bed this comfortable!   He hurt _everywhere_ but his shoulder, the right-side shoulder – almost made him pass out again if he tried to move it! At the very least he must have been shot there. Did he still have his arm on that side? He couldn't tell, the pain was too great to move any more.   Just trying made him woozy. He sighed and then did pass out again.

Ruth stood outside the sick room door for the eighth day in a row, for it was now Tuesday night, and she heard the incessant and desperate cries of the Major. For the last two days now, he had been tossing and turning and keeping them on their toes, getting more active as the time moved along. He would cry for Madeline. He would cry for Elizabeth. He would cry for help and shout the names of various officers and call for fire power or retreats. The doctor had authorized more medications to keep him from hurting himself with his thrashing about. But nothing stopped his continual distress. They now had a full-time male nurse, Ryan, in attendance, recommended by the doctor and he was at least allowing Jim and Henry to get some sleep. However, staff were loyal and often in the room after only a short amount of rest. Ruth could not remember the last time she had been to bed....probably Monday night over a week ago – yes that was when. She did sleep in the rocker for insignificant amounts of time and twice on the lounge for an hour.

The Major perspired so much, had urine accidents, and would accidently knock a teacup or something liquid out of someone's hands so his bed had to be changed repeatedly. Thankfully Ruth kept a separate folded sheet under his shoulders that caught most of such mess and was easier to change than the whole bed. He had begun to bleed from a number of lacerations and from his stubble of an arm, which also called for medicating and changes in linens. She had applied salve to prevent infection and bandaged it several times, sending the old wrappings to be burned. Staff had been sent to purchase bandages and more salve in quantity and it took them quite a time because the small store in the town did not have sufficient supply. Poor soul, she wanted him to live more than anything but would he? Was this a healing process or was he dying? She did not know and the doctor at this morning's visit admitted he did not either, the only good news being he did not have a high fever very often or very long at a time. Madeline's last days had been relatively quiet although she had moaned but not this thrashing and hollering! Ruth's own father had died with anger and intolerance of his condition fourteen years ago and this was the worst she had experienced since.

She did not want him to die! She had admired him from afar but never thought to be interested in him...not really caring for any of the men she had met....but now, well now may be different. Oh, botheration, this was awful! And poor Elizabeth, she looked twice her age and so very sad! Ruth must have dozed off, for by chimes of the hall clock almost an hour had passed. Now Ellie was tapping her on her sleeve. "Aunt Ruth, Aunt Ruth, wake up."
"Yes, Darling, what is it?"
"Father opened his eyes! He did, I assure you!"
"Well, that is very good. Did he seem to know where he was or recognize you?"
"He didn't look at me, but looked around the room some, and said 'Madeline?' then went back to sleep."
"Oh, good! At least we know he is cognizant of his marriage, even if not where he is right now or his condition! Come help me try to get some sweet tea and broth into him, Dear. Where is Ryan? "

"He went to the kitchen for something to eat, I believe. He hadn't broken his fast yet and had been awake most of the night. He said I must wake you if I needed help watching Father. Oh, I meant to tell you, the kitten is in the barn for a few days, Jim suggested it and I felt it was a good idea – better than him being shut up in the closet. I took him several days ago."

"Very wise for the kitten, Dear. You have been such a good nurse for your Father, too. I can't wait until he is alert enough to know what great help you have been. Can you imagine it is Wednesday already!"

With Elizabeth standing on a chair and helping to hold his head up, Ruth was able to get a half cup of warm, sweet tea into him a sip at a time. Then she did the same with chicken broth. He seemed cooperative, although not fully awake, but had no trouble swallowing or licking his lips. They both hoped that maybe today he would awaken enough to know them. He sighed as Ellie let him lay back again and they returned to their seats, Ellie with her book and Ruth closing her eyes to rest, although doubtful she would go to sleep.

Unbeknownst to them, Alfred was indeed waking up again. He was most confused. He glanced about him a bit, realizing he could only see out of one eye and that through a layer of bandages. Although the room looked vaguely familiar, even just peeking at it.

Well, it definitely wasn't the dirty, crowded military hospital, for sure and certain! Where was he? Had someone taken in soldiers to help them heal? Why did those curtains look familiar – or did they, maybe he wasn't seeing well enough to know? He wondered if he had seen them before, but how could that be…wasn't he in France, maybe he saw them before they bandaged his eyes? Wait - no, not France, an army hospital that was it! Well, no not an army hospital, not with nice curtains and such a fine bed. This wasn't a dirty cot – definitely not. A good mattress and clean sheets – well that was a change! Okay, let's regroup. Not a normal army hospital, maybe a house in France that was sympathetic to England and taking in English soldiers? Definitely hurt English soldiers – for he hurt in many places. There were no English army hospitals in France and no households who would likely take in an English officer who was badly hurt! Tarnation – what in the living hell had happened to him! The worst by far was his right arm! The whole arm hurt but when he tried to move the hand, nothing happened. Was it strapped down, maybe, or in a heavy bandage…why couldn't he move his right hand? Attempting to turn his head, and get a better look, he realized his neck hurt, his shoulder hurt, his chest was very heavy – like pneumonia maybe? Oh, Goodness! Trying to move his right arm was so painful he felt himself drifting into unconsciousness again. Just as he was

94

losing thought, did he feel a small cool hand on his left arm? However, he was too close to passing out to know what it was.

Ruth was waking up; she hadn't realized she had gone to sleep again. Evidently breakfast had relaxed her enough to shut her eyes for a bit. Ellie was standing close and looking at her with a very concerned expression. "I am awake Dear, is something the matter?"

"I believe Father was awake a little while, Aunt Ruth. He didn't speak but was trying to look at the window curtains despite his bandage, and frowning, and groaned when he tried to move his right shoulder. I believe he may be awakening!"

Ruth went over to the bed and straighten his covers somewhat and felt his head. Well, good news, hardly any fever! She raised his head and indicated Ellie should plump the pillow and together they succeeded. Maybe he would wake up soon. Even though emaciated, the Major was heavy to lift and she was cautious in her handling. She whispered to Ellie that they would stay quiet since it appeared he was sleeping and not moaning as he had been. She lifted Ellie onto her lap and they rocked together.

He hurt absolutely everywhere! He must have been severely injured but where was he now? He vaguely remembered being on the battlefield and bleeding profusely but trying his best to help several other

95

soldiers. Oh, yes, Randolph! Oh, God, Randolph. He had not been able to save Randolph. They had been friends even before the Army – just boys. Randolph was bleeding profusely from the chest. He had promised him to do something but he couldn't remember now what it was….maybe see his parents, although that didn't seem right, was there a wife? Well, that didn't seem correct either. What had he promised Randolph? Well, don't worry about Randolph right now, find out where you are and how badly you are injured – that's it – that's what to do! He tried moving his left leg and found he could – with great pain in the thigh, really great pain in the thigh. Heavens! Don't move that leg again, man! Botheration! Oh, try the other leg. Ahh, that one is better. It is very stiff and sore but it moves a little and nowhere near as hurtful as the left. Ok, now try the left arm, does it move? It seems to be able to but something is holding it? Maybe he is imagining that. Who would be on a battlefield holding his hand? Oh, remember you decided you weren't on a battlefield anymore. Maybe a nurse is there. She has really small, cool hands. Funny, thinking of that with so many other problems! He sighed and passed out.

Awakening again Alfred had not a single idea how long he had been unconscious that time, but he needed to check out his surroundings. Was he safe here? Well, he assumed so, no enemy would have him in such a great bed! Take stock of yourself, Major. Get with it! Ok, his legs were there, the left obviously hurt but the right in better condition. The feet moved, that was good, he would be able to walk most likely. Now the left arm was very stiff and the hand appeared to have a couple broken or dislocated fingers but it would do. Now what in tarnation was going on with his right arm? The shoulder hurt more than any pain he could ever remember – of course right now his memory wasn't that good – but it hurt terribly! What about the right hand, he couldn't tell, if it didn't move or just couldn't make it move.

He did not feel a hand on that side to touch his waist. Why couldn't he touch the right side of his waist? Oh, no! There was no hand there! Not even bandaged! He groaned. Oh, he was ruined! How could Madeline love him if his hand was gone? Well, stupid, she would love you anyway, you know that…just like you love her no matter what! Okay, keep checking.

He had been hit in the head, shot in the head or something because he had a headache worse than any ever before – well, he thought so anyway, who knew? He couldn't see anything but believed it was bandages – hopefully he wasn't blind! What a mess he was in! He wondered again where he was…He felt a cool small hand on his forehead. Oh, that felt so good even through the bandages! Someone gave him a drink of tea, very sweet and nice. Then a drink of chicken soup. Who was it? That is why the cool hand had moved to the back of his head and was holding his head to help him drink. He drank a lot of the tea, it tasted so good! He drank a lot of the chicken broth too! If that was the nurse she really had small hands! He passed out again.

"Oh, Darling you should have awakened me. Don't cry, baby. Don't cry. He did drink the tea and broth. And he didn't choke, so that is a very good sign. He will be so proud when he wakes and knows you have helped him so much!" She lifted Ellie onto her lap again.

The male nurse was gone for a rest and the room was quiet except for the heavy breathing from the bed. She rocked the chair and Ellie snuggled close. "We should go find some nourishment as soon as one of the men comes back. It is past nuncheon and we need to keep up our strength so we can help your Father! Would you eat come nuncheon for me?"

Ellie nodded solemnly. "I wish he would wake up just for a minute so I could tell him how I love him! Do you think he will wake this afternoon?"

"Well, let us hope so. He will hurt more while awake, but since he is taking the tea and broth so well, we can feed him some heartier chicken and dumpling soup and also some custard if he is really awake. We can order it while we eat our meal and then they can bring it when cooked. I hope he will remember who we are and where he is but we must not be distressed if he is confused. He was injured a long time ago and it may have affected him more than we would like." Ryan returned looking refreshed and suggested the "ladies" go and have some repast. Ruth grinned and nodded, taking Ellie's hand and walking to the kitchen to let them know they would be in the sunroom and telling staff what they wanted to eat to save them a trip just for information purposes. They also ordered some more substantial food for the patient, hoping he would be awake enough to eat it. When asked, they let staff know he had mumbled and seemed to wake for very short periods.

When the girl and her aunt were out of earshot staff discussed how awful and tired Ruth looked. Poor soul had not slept in many days except for short minutes in the rocker. Poor soul!
It was well past nuncheon time and twilight outside. Someone had put out some bread and the birds were feasting. Ellie slipped outside and broke off some of the flowers Henry had along the back fence. She brought them in and went to the kitchen for a pitcher with water. Doris brought their food and nuncheon was wonderful. Tasty and warm, just what they needed. Both ate well, and Ruth was so glad that the stress and concern for her father had not prevented Ellie from eating….she would need it if her father did awaken – for he would need a lot of care! Staff said

they would bring the Major's food shortly to his room so Ellie and Ruth headed back. Ellie hurried along carrying her flowers, obviously anxious to see her father and if he would wake up and know her.

Ryan told them the Major had been mumbling and moving but not the frantic tossing around of before. She felt the patient was about to wake up. Ellie took the chair and put it right beside the head of the bed and sat down to watch her father. She was rewarded because shortly after she got situated, he did indeed wake up. Mumbling, he said, "Hello, is anyone there? Where am I, please?"

"Oh, Father, it is Ellie, Father. I am right here beside you. You have been very ill but we have been helping you. Do you want a drink of tea, Father?"

"Ellie, is that you, my Ellie?"

"Yes, Father, I am right here! I am so glad you are awake! We, Aunt Ruth and I, have been giving you tea and broth and wiping your brow. And Big Jim is here and helping too!"

"Oh, I am home! Oh, Ellie, Darling! Where is Madeline? Call your Mother for me, Dear."

Ellie sobbed and Ruth rushed up. "Alfred, it is Ruth here. I cannot call for Madeline. How are you feeling? Do you hurt anywhere that we can help?"

"My right arm is awful and my left leg too, but my head is the worst. I have a very bad headache. You say you cannot bring Madeline? That is unusual, she does not often go out. When will she be back?"

"Oh, Alfred, she cannot come, dearest. She is not with us anymore. She was so very ill, Dear. She has passed away."

He was so shocked he couldn't speak but heard Ellie sobbing. "Oh, Ruth! Oh, Ellie, Dear! What in the world has happened?"

Trying to speak even while crying, Ellie stammered that her Mother had been ill for most of a year with cholera. "We missed you, Father. We missed you so much! I prayed you would come back to me. I am so very glad you are here, Father!"

"Oh, Baby. I am so very sorry. You know I loved your Mother dearly, do you not? I am beyond sad at her death, Dear. I am so very sorry. Now here I am a great burden, too!"

"NO! NO! Do not say that Father. I have prayed you would return. Now you are here and Aunt Ruth and I will nurse you. As if to prove her words, Ruth supported his head and gave him chicken broth recently left by kitchen staff, richer with minced chicken. Then she followed with sweet cool tea. "I have so many injuries. I am sorry to be such a burden." "Now you listen to me Major Alfred Masters, we will not hear such! We will see you well and that's a fact." Just as he drifted back to sleep, they heard him chuckle.

CHAPTER SEVEN

The whole house was alive with discussion. "The Master was awake!" "Ruth said he would get better." "Ellie was up on the bed with him and his left arm was around her." "He drank all the heavier chicken broth in the pintcup." "They told him about Lady Madeline." Hardly any cooking got done for an hour or so, they were so busy with happy gossip.

As he slept, Elizabeth also took a little nap, close to his side. What a pretty pair, her hair in braids with rag ties, his head bandaged, arm skinned up and fingers crooked but content to be together.

Ruth sat close and Jim took the liberty, while Ellie was asleep to clean up the master's private area and put down more towels. Ruth figured after this nap they would manage to get him to stand if Ryan or one of the other men came to help also. They could change his bed better and it would be good for his blood to be up a bit.

Well, she sighed, he knew who they were, he drank a good bit of his lunch, he seemed to be in less pain, and the worst was over by telling him about Madeline. Maybe this evening would be the best in way over a week. Ellie certainly looked happier.

True to Ruth's expectations, after a nice nap, the Major again woke up. For a second he had to get his bearings but looking down at Ellie still napping close to his side, he grinned at her and signed with contentment that he had gotten to see her again.

When he had been conscious in the hospital, he had doubted he would ever get back home. Although homecoming was certainly not what he had hoped. His dearest Madeline – gone? Oh, Lord, why did you do that to us…I loved her so. They had fun and loved each other so much.

Well, he would do better by Ellie than his in-laws had done by Madeline. He would see she was happy at least. He would not force her to stay in the house and read as his wife had been required to do as a youth. He would find out how she was now she was older. It had been almost a year since he had seen her but she was a beauty and so kind. What a lovely daughter we made Madeline.

Ellie woke with a start and then realized her father's arm was around her and she reached her little face up and kissed him beneath his bandage.

He chuckled and kissed her forehead. "Sugar, I think, if there are enough men around to help me, I will try to stand up. Can you get down from the bed for a bit while I try?"

"Oh, Yes Papa! I will and both Jim and Henry are here to help you. I will go with Ruth and we will see what can be fixed for your supper. Since your head is bandaged is your jaw hurt, can you chew?"

"Well, Sweets, I am not certain at this point what I can and cannot do. But we will see. My mouth does not hurt overmuch, so I do not believe my jaw is broken nor my teeth knocked out. My main complaint, besides the missing arm, is my one leg does hurt a great deal, so I am not certain how much of my weight it will hold. I do have a severe pain in the right side of my head but that should not interfere with eating. I certainly don't weigh what I used to…just call me skin and bones. Are you planning to fatten me up?"

She giggled as intended and jumped down.

Ruth rushed up and lifted his head and shoulders, putting several pillows behind him – to give his body a little lift. As Big Jim and Henry approached, she and Ellie said they would see him shortly and left the room to give him privacy.

They were both so anxious about him, without telling each other, but both wondering: What if he fell? What if he couldn't walk, What if he got worse?

They checked with the kitchen to see if any special food was in the preparation for the Major and finding staff were doing everything they could think of; they both grinned. What a nice surprise, how kind staff were to go to so much extra trouble. A souffle, a creamed mushroom soup, and a vanilla bean custard.

Ellie told them he was trying to stand up with the help of Big Jim and Henry. She shared that it worried her, should he fall or the broken leg not hold him and did more damage. They assured her, just as Ruth had that the men would be very careful and protective of him – both being very tall and strong, they would prevail.

"Darling, I am not certain just where the break on his leg is – if it is high, near his body, then it may be a while before he can walk or sit on a wheeled chair. We will prevail but I don't want you disappointed if he must stay in bed quite a long time yet – okay?"

Ellie nodded seriously and said she could run errands for him and bring the kitten and tell him about the piano and tell him about the horse riding and tell him she had progressed two books in her arithmetic and have him quiz her on her spelling – if he could see well enough that is. She stopped to draw a breath and Ruth laughed at her, making her smile really wide.

"Oh, Aunt Ruth, I will be careful to not bother him over much, really I will, but isn't it just grand that he woke up and knows us."

'It is, indeed, my girl. We will help him get better."

Jim and Henry looked like storm clouds when the girls returned from eating. They turned away from the door as the girls entered but not before Ruth noticed. Obviously they didn't want Ellie to see their

105

displeasure. Alfred was laying back on the bed as white as a sheet and breathing heavily. Oh, Dear! This did not bode well. Motioning with her head toward the hallway, Jim went out and she followed.

"What in the world is the matter? Can he not walk, what do we need to do for him?"

"The stupid Army doctors, oh, Ma'am it is so awful, they have set his leg wrong. No wonder he is in such pain with it. We need a doctor and probably a surgeon as soon as ever possible. Can you get the doctor here immediately Miss Ruth? And see if a surgeon is available in the area?"

"We will indeed, I suggest we keep Henry in here to help and have Ryan stay with him too. You will ride to Dr. Ormond immediately and tell him what you feel is happening to the leg. Surgery may be needed and you should mention that. Please leave as soon as you can."

She did not do this lightly. Death during surgery was commonplace and it was an awful decision. They would probably need to rebreak the leg. Oh, she just had a terrible thought – what if he lost the leg? Oh, Dear God, please don't let that happen! If it was the only thing to keep him alive, then so be it, but she prayed not.

While Dr. Ormond was here she would get him to check Alfred's head wound as well. She hadn't removed the bandage because other matters seemed more pressing but it concerned her.

Alfred was not asleep and she went to him and asked if he thought Ellie practicing the piano would bother him...the piano being in the old study, now principally a music room. He grinned broadly and said no it would not bother him at all. Ruth explained that she had just started lessons and calling it music was optimistic. He laughed and said for her to play by all means, it didn't matter the quality he would like to hear it and hoped it carried enough to his room that he would be able to.

Ellie was excited but reluctant because of her inability to play well. But Ruth encouraged her.

She danced down the hall and entered the music room. Ruth saw her draw in a couple deep breaths and then she took her seat on the bench and started with some scales, which she did flawlessly. This seemed to encourage her and she began with the abbreviated tunes the teacher had given her, which made her feel like she was really playing something.

Typical of a child, she was soon involved in her playing to the extent she was not hesitant anymore and Ruth was impressed at the quality. Of course, there were mistakes it had only been such a short while. She quietly slipped out and back to the sick room.

The men were supporting the Major on the side of the bed and Dr. Ormond was examining the leg carefully. Ruth could tell the pain must be pretty intense from the tight, white line Alfred's lips were making but he didn't say a word of complaint.

Feeling deeply, they all heard Alfred gasp, but the Doctor said it was not as bad as it looked – although they were correct it was not healing straight. He would get in touch with a surgeon today and see if that learned man thought anything could be done.

As requested by Ruth, he removed the head bandage and it was nasty underneath but the healing looked fairly straight. He withdrew some ointment from his medical bag that he recommended be applied four times a day and the old washed off with very warm and soapy water before each reapplication.

Alfred said he was glad for the removal of the bandage, which allowed him to see much better and would it need to be replaced? The doctor said it would not as long as the raw area was kept clean and free of foreign matter that might stick to the wound. And someone would need to cut his hair frequently to keep it out of the way.

All of a sudden the Doctor appeared to be listening and asked who was learning to play the piano. When told it was none other than Elizabeth he commented that she certainly was learning quickly. Alfred agreed and said he enjoyed hearing it mistakes and all. Ruth couldn't wait to tell Ellie of the compliments from both of them.

Ruth was preparing a clean soap cloth for Alfred's head and before the doctor was out the door she was gently rubbing away the old, dried blood and dead skin. She heard the in-drawn breath of the patient but assured him it was necessary to get it completely clean before she added the medication.   He bit his lip and nodded.

Finishing and cleaning her hands well, she then cut his hair quite short and applied the medication. Alfred said he had expected it to hurt but it felt cool and tingly but not bad at all.

Alfred thanked her for all the attention she provided and also thanked the men for their constant care and aiding him to move about some which did indeed seem to help his whole body.

As Ruth finished up, she turned, probably too quickly and slumped to the floor.   Everyone in the room panicked.   Alfred tried to get up, both the men there ran to that side of the bed, Elizabeth, who had come back from piano playing, sobbed.   Ruth was more than embarrassed.   She grabbed the mattress to help herself up and said it was perhaps a lack of sleep.

Alfred asked when she had been to bed last, and she hesitated but couldn't lie to him and said well, she believed: nine days ago, or was it ten?

"My God, Woman, are you trying to kill yourself! Gentlemen, please see she is escorted to her room immediately.   Ascertain she does not fall on the stairs."

109

CHAPTER EIGHT

The whole house was abuzz! Ruth had fallen, Ruth had not slept in nine days, what would Ellie do without Ruth, what would any of them do without Ruth, what would the Major do without Ruth…and on and on.

Big Jim was amazed at his feelings. When he had seen her slump, he had rushed his best to help her. She was so caring and he had watched from the barn and the house as she helped Elizabeth with enjoyment like the horses and piano but also less enjoyable things like studies – even the arithmetic that Ellie was not too pleased at doing. A genuinely good woman. What would the household do without her? And her nursing skills with both Madeline and now the Major were superb.

No one could possibly have helped Lady Madeline any more than Ruth. She had been by the bedside for months. Bathing, reading, measuring medication, soothing her in a calm and sweet way.

Although the whole household was thinking along similar lines, none realized the Major was also assessing the petite woman, who had tirelessly tended him for so many hours without regard for herself.…HE had to be the reason she had not slept. He had known Ruth in passing ever since he had first met Maddie. She had been the very young cousin really just a girl then but always helpful and so kind to his sweetheart, who had endured endless restriction at the hands of a no-good father and a mother who tried to make her life better by restricting everything around her – of course except the one thing she wanted to restrict and couldn't, her 'ner'do'well husband!

He always wished he could make life better for Maddie, but the upbringing had damaged her. Now faced with something happening to Ruth, he realized how much difference she had made in the household. She was the force behind this happy estate and his very happy daughter.

He had no idea what his dear wife would have done without her. She was really almost the only friend Maddie had enjoyed. Family only wanting money.

He told her she was too generous but she just shrugged and said it was just lying in the bank, why not let someone enjoy the money. Unlike the others, Ruth never took any payment - refusing adamantly.

He missed his Maddie. They had the best talks and intimacy and shared everything about their lovely daughter. He would have been happy to have created another child, but they hadn't and so they had doted on Ellie. And what a reward she was! But somewhere in his mind he had to admit that Ruth had really brought out the best in Ellie. She was making her an independent person and so accomplished by offering her horseback riding and music.

He must make every effort to get himself well again. He would have some handicaps for sure and certain. His arm was gone, nothing to be done about that. His one leg was indeed in awful shape, but he would prevail. He would walk again and learn to write with his left hand. He would not be a burden to either Ellie or Ruth.

How he would love to ride a horse again. The last he had been on one was in the army just before they were taken over by the French. His unit suffered such terrible losses and while he was unconscious the Frenchies had stolen his military mount. Of course, he hadn't been able to ride well even had he found a stray horse but he could have managed to seat given the opportunity. He had continued to command his men and keep them from being captured by hiding and crawling and fighting hand to hand. Whatever it took, he tried it, and finally another unit had reached them and they were returned to England.

Huh, Ruth had read to him some were writing that he was to be awarded a gold star and possibly promoted, but he didn't want any of it. He had failed to protect his men, so many losses, so much heartache, so much injury. He did not deserve any recognition. He had lost Randolph...he would never get over seeing that!

He understood that the French had lost many more. Their ranks had been devastated, although being on their own soil they did get better supplies of food but the English had superior weapons and fighting ability. What awful losses on both sides. Poor Randolph. Poor Henry, Poor Richmond, poor everyone! Hopefully this would be the last of the wars with France. They had thought them finished before but unfortunately Napoleon had again launched this series of battles. This time the high command felt the wars were at last over, my he certainly hoped so!

He finally dozed off again. He dreamed of battles, fighting his covers until Big Jim woke him, got him straighten out in bed and gave him some medication. After a warm face wash and the pillow turned to the cool side, he again drifted off to sleep, hoping he wouldn't refight the war in his dreams yet again.

Ellie had napped and awakening, looked for Ruth then realized that Ruth was still asleep. So, Ellie skipped downstairs to check on Papa

He was propped up on a number of pillows and Jim had braced the tray on two stacks of books, making a little table and Dad was laughing and able to feed himself with only a little spilling using the left arm.

Jim kept studying the bed with a puzzled expression. "What is wrong with my bed?" asked Alfred. "Nothing, Sir, with the bed that is, but I can certainly make a tray that would be better than that pillow and book contraption! As soon as my replacement comes I will go to the barn and construct what I think will work really well and not be so havey skavey.

About that time Paul returned and Jim said he would be back in an hour or so. Ellie watched him leave and wondered what he could possibly do in a horse barn that would help her father?

As Ellie read her book and sipped her tea, having thanked staff for her luncheon that she hastily ate, she again wondered what Jim could be doing in the barn so long. It had been over an hour at least. She was always curious about things. She hoped it wasn't impolite or anything. Aunt Ruth said it was how you learned, by being – what was the word? – oh, inquisitive! That sounded like a good word to remember.

Her wait was about another quarter hour when Jim came back in smiling all over himself. He gently took the existing tray from the Major and put it aside and handed the books that had supported it to Ellie. Alfred had finished eating almost everything, which would please Ruth when she returned. Jim then straightened the bedding and asked the Major if he could bring something in?

"Certainly, Son, whatever do you have?"

Grinning Jim reached around the door and brought in a tray but it had short legs and the edge of the tray was tacked with leather keeping it from being rough. He demonstrated how it would go over the Major's lap to hold his meal without the plate or tray having to be steadied.

"Well, look here! This is just fine. They could have used these in the hospital, someone tipped their food over almost every meal. How smart you are. Where did you get the nice leather edging?"

"Oh, I had an extra belt that was wider than I cared for and I used part of that. You will notice it doesn't quite go all the way around but should make the edge more comfortable where it touches you."

"Thank you Jim, this is very nice. It is exactly what he needs. Thank you!" Said Ruth who had come through the door while everyone was looking at the tray with legs.

"Well, did you get a good rest, my Dear?"

"Yes, Alfred, I did indeed. I am sorry to have deserted you so long but it was very nice to lie on a bed with pillows – I was quite tired of the rocking chair." And she laughed her musical laugh.

Noises were heard in the hall and Thomas Adams announced: "Doctor Ormond and Dr. Drewsbury."

Oh, my, thought Ruth, what a serious pair. Well, she hoped that seriousness foretold the ability to study Alfred's leg and come up with a workable solution for correcting the poor misshapen thing.

Jim hurried to remove the tray and dishes and folded back the covers. There was that awful looking leg. Obviously not straight and purple and just terrible.
"Ladies if you will excuse us please, we will tend to this and call you when you may return. We will have to turn him and take off his gown. It would be best if you waited elsewhere."

"Yes, Dr. Ormond, we will be in the music room, please send someone for me if I can help. Alfred, I so hope they can do something that will alleviate all that pain." Taking Elizabeth's hand, they left the room.
Jim stood by to help move the patient or hold him still as they worked on him, which would undoubtedly be very, very painful.
In the music room, Ruth encouraged Ellie to play something, knowing the music would help drown out any noises made by the Major, when she was certain moving that leg would be excruciatingly painful. She was not mistaken and even with the music and two rooms away, they could occasionally hear the moans and shouts of the Major as the leg was straightened or examined. Ellie was crying but continued playing as asked, hoping the music would somehow soothe her Father. After the last particularly awful uproar, it got very quiet and Ellie asked if they needed to go to the room and check on her father. Ruth told her no, not until they were sent for, but he had probably

116

gone to sleep…a lie but she didn't want to tell the child that he had probably passed out from the pain.

It seemed like forever that they waited, Ellie played, and Ruth paced. Both silently prayed. Surgery would have been one option, she was thinking, but in his state of health and with no operating room and questionably sterile conditions, she felt surgery would probably not be recommended. As many people died during surgery as survived it, so the safest was probably what they were doing.

Finally, Big Jim came and said they could return to the bedroom now. The doctors were preparing to leave and would like to speak with Ruth for a minute. When they entered the Major was indeed unconscious and a gray color but breathing almost normally, Thank Heaven! Ellie sobbed, but Ruth pointed out the breathing and that she would return in a bit after talking with the doctors and getting instructions on how to best help Alfred.

The news was better than she might have thought but still not wonderful. They had rebroken the leg at the small point it had been splintered apart and healed incorrectly, surgically aligning the bones and flesh, and restitching the area closed. Thankfully, just a small area had been improperly done, where the bone was crooked; not much change needed. The bone aligned – she didn't want to ask how they did that – it sounded horribly painful, obviously including

117

rebreaking a piece! The surgeon had sewn it shut, medicated it, and bandaged it tightly but not so tight it would cut off circulation of course - securely enough that tossing and turning in his sleep would not dislodge the splint and bandage. They felt it was as good as could be done and better than expected. His groin would be sore and need salve applied regularly. He had been given considerable laudanum and he should sleep for some time

Alfred was <u>not</u> to try to walk with any pressure on that leg for three weeks! That was most important and with no full weight on the injured leg until ten weeks. The doctors would visit periodically. It was not guaranteed that he would not lose the leg. Such reattaching was often not successful, particularly since much time had passed from the initial injury…they would just have to see what happened, it was the new break that would heal. Affirming that Dr. Ormond would be by in two weeks to check on him but come get him or send a runner if they had any earlier concerns. The good doctor telling Ruth that he was amazed the surgeon had been able to only have to reset a very small piece of bone given the awful damage on the battlefield. Just a bit needed to be rebroken and straightened with splinters removed, he didn't realize such a thing could be done. Hopefully the Major's body would regrow some of it, however that happened! And please keep the skin area where it was stitched up very clean. Of particular caution was if the area drained a yellow liquid or the pain increased. He may still lose the leg, but they had done all they could under the circumstances. The leg would never be correct but if it continued to heal as now tied up, it would be useable to a degree. They must realize it had been too long and the bone may not repair itself. But the doctors had done all they could, sorry to say. He would have a limp and weakness but they tried to save the leg. Alfred was to use a crutch **always**, regardless of his pride. Once he was allowed up, they could devise a leather bandage to support the injury.

Ellie was assured that her father was sleeping fairly comfortably, she agreed to Ruth's suggestion that they go to the reading library and do her lessons and then Ruth would read to her from one of the new Jane Austen books. Ellie, although reluctant to be away from her Father so long, agreed and with the enticement of Ruth reading a novel to her, she tackled her lessons with eager anticipation of finishing post haste.
Ellie did her lessons as well as could be expected given her mind wandered to her poor father with every page.

The Middle Years – Growing Up and Exploring Out

CHAPTER NINE

The next many months, saw the Major indeed improve. He was up trying to walk on the first day allowed. His appetite better and starting to take an interest in various things on the estate. Unfortunately, even with the adjustments made by the surgeon to his left leg, it had not healed very well, and although not amputated, it would not hold his weight without a crutch or cane employed, plus of course the leather binding that had been recommended by the surgeon, designed by Ruth and made by Jim.

However, he *was* up and about. Ruth had sewn some canvas, making her fingers bleed, but it was a wrap going around the upper leg with leather straps for over his shoulders and gave the leg additional support besides the cane and leather binding. Alfred said it indeed did comfort him to have more support and thanked her profusely.

After several months, he had started riding again for very short periods, using a mounting block, but the canvas wrap helped protect the injured leg and yet still allowed him to use his foot to help guide his very large and faithful horse, Storm, which he had procured from a horse stable recommended by Lord Baden to their horse man, Jim. It was a most successful animal – not at all skittish or unstable as its name might imply.

Alfred had corresponded with former members of his outfit and gotten back a large number of letters. Most made him shake his head in disbelief because they credited him with saving a vast number of his regiment. He had graciously refused his commission, saying his injuries would not allow him to serve and he could not in all good consciousness accept an advancement when he could no longer command. Parliament had sent a formal honor, signed by members, and accepted proudly by the Major at the insistence of Elizabeth and Ruth. Elizabeth herself framing it for hanging in the library.

He was visited by so many that it was good Ruth kept a ledger or he would most probably forget a large number of them all.

A boy he had known, now a grown man by the name of Sir Jonathan Baden (who had recommend the horse stable) corresponded and introduced by letter his wife, the sister of a boy he had also known. The sister was Lady Jane Morton now Baden and they had the big Summerwood Estate twenty miles away but encouraged Major Masters to visit any time at his convenience. They had all been children to his adult self but such nice families.

Jane Baden's brother, Lord Edward Morton, though younger was closer in age as the Major remembered. Edward now ensconced in Parliament where he had distinguished himself in an honorable manner regarding thefts to aid Napoleon and along with Lord Richardson, whose father had served in the wars, and been a good friend and commander of Alfred's.

Lords Baden and Ricardson insisted many others from Parliament had been on the committee that worked to prevent the treason of goods to France. Alfred remembered the two boys as smart scoundrels who liked to fish and torment some young girl with blond hair. He had never known who the girl was but wondered from the letter if Mistress Baden, who had assisted with the finding of illegal arms going to France, could possibly be that same sister of Lord Morton he had known as a small girl. Although it didn't seem likely given her youth and distance from London.

As a few years of time passed, Ellie had her thirteenth birthday, an actual party, completed happily and she enjoyed it tremendously. She had invited a few neighbors who had been kind to her mother and some who had written to her father lately. The party was indeed wonderful, noisy, and enjoyed by all.

Ruth did not know a lot of those attending but at once liked very much Lady Baden and Lady Morton, whose two small children played in the solarium and looked like duplicates of their parents. Lord Richardson, a supreme commander during the war and his son came and that alone made Alfred happy. They discussed the war only briefly – none wanting to rehash the horror. Alfred thanked Lord Morton and the others for their successful effort to prevent more cannons and arms to get to France for their war effort. All seemed to credit the smiling, petite Lady Baden for much of the success of that action, but the Major still did not understand how a little young woman like that could have helped. Ruth told him she would have someone explain later. It was likely a most interesting story.

Elizabeth had almost given up hope of Ruth and her father making a love match, which she had so wished and believed Ruth liked him very, very well! She knew it was not really her business but could tell they each watched the other when not aware she was paying attention and seemed so agreeably attuned. They discussed not only estate things but music, plays, read books together, and rode as long as his leg could stand it. My, it would be nice if they married!

Alfred also realized how important Ruth had become to him…of course to his daughter always… but to him personally. She was not only lovely to look at but the kindest and most considerate he had ever met

123

– even treating staff better than his wife or anyone else he knew had ever done.

They had begun sitting next to each other at meals instead of across the table. They rode together, read together, sat together while Ellie played the piano. Just seemed happy near to each other in general. Elizabeth was so very pleased!

She was thinking about her father and Aunt Ruth. Now that his "bad" leg did not hurt so terribly they could move about more and were friends.

Ellie had stayed with staff one day while they went to the attorney offices, where her father could learn of all the bequests made by her mother, Madeline, and that he had inherited considerable wealth in the process. When they returned he was aghast at the happenings and discussed it again with Ruth over dinner while Ellie listened and smiled thinking he felt the same as she and Ruth had on their visit.

As weeks passed, she had realized that her father was finally getting over his sadness at the loss of her mother and did like Ruth – A LOT! One day, when only the two were riding together, her father asked: "Elizabeth would you mind terribly if I courted Ruth?" She almost fell off her horse! "Oh, Father, I thought you would never say such but I am so very pleased. She has never looked at anyone else the way she does you. Did you not realize she cares for you?"

He shook his head "no", blushing profusely. "Well, I suggest that you do something about it then, Sir." Said his wise daughter with a grin and then laughter. Within a few days, it became apparent that the Major had started his pursuit of Ruth because a box of chocolates arrived, roses arrived and they started even holding hands on occasion.

Ruth and Alfred had discussed their mutual affection and he was concerned about his "ragged state" as he called it but, of course, Ruth told him it did not matter in the least. Much to her surprise, after one of his infrequent trips to London with some friends, he presented her with an engagement ring of a beautiful sapphire to "match her eyes" and they planned to be married in the fall. They were indeed most happy and their "daughter" not the least of it.

After all it had been over four years and the engagement ring was exactly what Ellie wanted them to do. Two of the years were taken up with the Major learning to walk using crutches but with much pain. Taking great care of his arm stub which had been inclined to serious infection for the better part of a year. Plus, occasional bouts of gout and severe headaches. He seemed to feel he was second rate and it made Ellie sad, but she understood his frustration.

On a pleasant fall day, as they came in from riding, Alfred and Ruth wondered who Elizabeth was talking to in the music room and it sounded like two

125

people were playing the piano…one accomplished and one not so much!

As they entered Lady Adrienne Moore stood up laughing and said that Elizabeth was trying to teach her son, Thomas, to play. He did not do very well but was getting better than all the paid lessons they had given him. They had arrived as Ellie was practicing and so been invited by her to join in, she explained. Alfred said it was probably the enticement of the teacher and Ruth gasped, but Lady Moore seemed very amused and nodded her head in agreement.

"We apologize, Miss Roberts and Major Masters, for coming unannounced, but we had come from London and were to pass right by here so thought, if you didn't mind we would stop for a minute. I wanted to say that we will definitely be at the church in two weeks for your wedding. I had sent my reply but mails what they are I wanted to mention it to you today. We are so very pleased for you!"

"Thank you, I hope everything goes according to plan. I am quite nervous – not about marriage to Alfred of course, but about the social aspect of the day. It appears everything is on schedule and with Lady Baden helping, I am certain nothing will be amiss. That Lady could organize a dozen weddings the same week and they would all be just fine – her four estates and child not withstanding!"

Adrienne laughed again and said that was for sure and certain. After all she had almost single-handedly stopped the load of illegal arms going to France. Had protected and nursed her husband – before they were courting - when his life was in danger and there were a number of incidents in London where she was attacked by scoundrels and one where she saved a girl at a wedding…she didn't have all the details but it was quite the talk of the Ton at the time.

"I had heard some rumors but would love to know more." Said Alfred.

"Oh, do we have time now? I am certain I can tell you about the arms shipment, for my husband, although not part of the parliamentary group involved, was so awe struck that he loves telling the story – quite unusual but proven true by the very outcome of the whole thing."

"If you will, please, wait a minute and I will call for staff and wash my hands. Won't you both stay for nuncheon?" Asked Ruth.

"Well, we are so much trouble, and to come unannounced is so rude. Are you certain you are not too tired?"

"Oh, no indeed! We ride several times a week and it seems to invigorate us. It is so pleasant, if it isn't raining, although I have been known to ride and get wet. I'll be right back." And bowing she left the room with Alfred looking after her with affection.

"While we are waiting, Father, we have been practicing one of my favorites…Listen to us, will you?"

"Certainly, Elizabeth."

"I am starting him on Wolfgang Mozart's Nanneri's Book – this is Minute in F and I am working on Allegro in C at other times when I practice. They are good starters – which I believe Mozart intended for his younger sister, Papa."

Although not a student of classical music therefore not Mozart, Alfred could tell immediately from the lyrical notes that his daughter knew. And even the untutored Tyson was not doing too badly at the accompanying part. Well, tarnation! He was a grown man and tearing up at a little bit of piano. Well, it wasn't the piano so much as the fact his daughter was growing up – as much as he hated to admit it.

Ruth started back hesitating and watching the piano pair. She was with Doctor Ormond.

As the piece came to an end and Adrienne, Alfred and Ruth clapped. Dr. Ormond came forward and said: "Oh, Elizabeth, thank you so much. I had not heard that played since my sister took piano lessons many years ago. I miss her terribly. Oh, don't look so sad, she is fine at her last letter but now married and living in somewhere in America called Baltimore. Her husband owns a shipping fleet. I hope the war between the "states" and England didn't bankrupt him but I guess it is over."

Ruth made introductions, crediting Dr. Ormond with healing Alfred and being a stalwart doctor and friend. "Oh, you do yourself an injustice, Madam, it was YOU who were the catalyst for Alfred healing. I only provided occasional guidance. Good morning everyone. I apologize for interrupting but had just been to the Mitchell estate down the road and was to let these good people know that I will be most honored to attend their wedding." he said, laughing.

At that Lady Moore, set her teacup aside, stood and asked" "Is there anything that I can do, Ruth?"

"Why thank you so much, but staff have been wonderful and Lady Baden is helping so things are a whirlwind but I believe finalized at last. We will see you in two weeks."

"Oh, please wait, don't go!" Alfred said immediately. "You have not told me about the role of Lady Baden in the defeat of Napoleon. I really would like to hear if it won't delay you too much. After all I had an interest in that struggle and gave body parts."

Both Ruth and Adrienne gave a horrified gasp and Alfred apologized but said it was easier to laugh at his disablement than to moan over it.

Dr. Ormond spoke up and said he had heard rumors that somehow Lady Baden had affected some kind of information that was helpful in the war and would

129

like to hear the details if he wasn't out of line in asking? He had wondered if it could be true, she being so young and living so far from London.

Elizabeth rang for a servant and ordered more light nuncheon. Ruth said: "Everyone have a seat, please. I believe the time has come for this information. We have bandied about this long enough....please share anything you know, Lady Moore."

"Well, as you probably already know, Jane err... Lady Baden, has a brother Edward, Lord Morton, who is in parliament. It seems Edward and several other members – I apologize for not remembering more but I am certain Lord Richardson (the younger one) and Lord Adams were among them - had discovered that there were missing funds of some note from the coffers of Parliament. Evidently boys who were aids to Lord Morton had also discovered the possible culprit, another Lord, was using some of the ill-gotten gains to purchase cannon, guns, ammunition and so forth.

Now of course it was not for the English navy. He would not be authorized to do so and not even part of the Admiralty. Therefore, it was thought that such were being collected to sell and the probable source of such arms would be either France or America – with France the likely object since the return of Napoleon was a hot rumor at the time and the difficulty with the States almost over."

"Why that is treason!" said Alfred Masters interrupting with consternation.

"It is indeed", added Doctor Ormond.

"Yes, well at this stage it was but a rumor and although Lord Morton and several others were certain of the missing funds, they could only surmised the use and location of the activity. Now the logical next step was IF such was missing, where in the world would it be? How could such large items as cannon be hidden? The men involved, using some of their hired help and much time and energy had searched maps, existing foundries, and known large sailing vessels – all without any discovery of wrongdoing. They were alarmed but helpless to prevent any such sale or treasonous activity without more information. Also, they couldn't find a port suitable for clandestine shipping."

"Now the interesting part. Lord Morton had talked with his sister, Lady Jane Baden, on several subjects and finally she had challenged him on what in the name of sense (I quote her) was the matter with him lately and his father-in-law too was acting very strange. Both worried, off their feed, and generally morose.

Finally, swearing her to the utmost secrecy, Lord Edward Morton explained to his sister the missing war equipment and the frustrated searches for where it may be. They did not feel enough time had gone for it to be out of the country yet, nor was Lord Irving showing any newfound wealth…therefore maybe they could prevent this tragedy if they only knew how and where. Of course, keeping their searches secret. It had been assured it was not in any of the ships and ports they had investigated. It must be somewhere less frequented.

Well, like leading a horse to water, this led Lady Baden to study the situation. The Lady is remarkably intelligent you know! She kept remembering something from her childhood – a book she thought, that described a hidden inlet on the coast. Now it all sounds havey skavey in the extreme – does it not? Our coastline is so many leagues long, which didn't discourage her. Jane, being Jane, knew her childhood book was at her father's house in the attic. So, she went on the hunt for it. Finding books including the one of the boy explorer.

She reread it and immediately went back to her current home and to Jonathan's study, withdrawing his naval maps. She became so excited, as Jonathan tells it, he could hardly understand her for she kept saying over and over: 'It is REAL, it EXISTS!' Calming her, Jonathan asked her to explain what in tarnation was in existence and real. She stated the hidden inlet and then showed him that indeed according to the child's book there was room for one large sailing vessel hidden from the normal shipping areas near Bosc in the childhood book she remembered. And further astonishment, it was shown on the maps that it was indeed there and a foundry adjacent.

Well, I see time is passing, so to make a long story short...that is exactly where the contraband was. An improperly licensed and registered large ship in a single width slip and next to an old but reopened cannon factory. With great trepidation and with Jonathan's encouragement, she sent the book to Edward. Now listen to this....she didn't just mail it in a paper to Sir Edward Morton...no indeed, she did not. She knew from her conversations with her brother that they were worried they would be discovered by the culprits and had kept things as secretive as possible but were still concerned they were being watched.

Of course, this didn't stop Jane. Knowing she better not use the normal post; she secreted the book between two other childhood books and forwarded them to a friend of her brother's wife. Anyway, not mailed to his house in case it was being watched. The receiver was instructed to wrap it in baby-gift paper as Lord Morton and his wife had just birthed a child. and delivered by this friend as a baby gift.

Lord Thompson and Lord Morton were kidnapped and almost killed by the scoundrels who had surmised they may be discovered. Other members of the Ton – including Lord Richardson and Lord Adams and I don't remember who else, came to their rescue after one of the two boys working for Lord

133

Morton had seen him abducted. And the ladies figured Lord Thompson was also since he had not come home either! Assuming they would be taken to the same illegal ship, they found them and everything worked out. They were rescued, the culprits caught, and the contraband not used by France. They all made a parade of coming back and taking the scoundrels directly to the prison under the watch of Lord "Augie" Augustus Hendrickson."

Gasping she sat down firmly on the settee, quite proud she had remembered enough of the tail to share it with the major and the doctor.

"Well, what a page in history, what a great relief! We had trouble enough beating the Frenchies without adding more arms and cannons. Oh, thank you for telling me. I must talk to Lady Baden when I see her at our wedding. How very smart she must be....and a good memory. I must remember to never anger her for she would undoubtedly not forget." Alfred said with a laugh.

Leaving Alfred wondering at the intelligence of Lady Baden. Doctor Ormond, Adrienne and her son had left. Since Alfred was frowning, Ruth promised to get all the information for him regarding their new friend Lady Jane Baden and how she managed the naval discovery, had earlier saved Jonathan, had any number of bad experiences herself with outlaws, and helped run the biggest set of estates in the area.

CHAPTER TEN

Elizabeth was so excited she could hardly contain herself! This was the day...the day she had wanted to come for several years. Ruth would be her mother and her father would have a companion that would make him laugh, visit people and people come to the Glass Castle to visit them. She was as certain as anything it was an absolutely perfect marriage.

The day was lovely, with warm but not hot sun, a slight breeze, and a temperature not requiring any heavy wraps or boots or scarves!

Being maid of honor, she took the duties very seriously. She had great help, with staff doing absolutely everything possible to facilitate the event – and a most luscious luncheon planned at the Castle for after the ceremony. Lady Jane Baden, in her inimitable way had organized the church. Then the ladies Adrienne Moore, Helen Randolph, Caroline Thompson and Judith Richardson had all done their part to make this extra special as well. Doing flowers, stacking presents, loaning silver, dishes, chairs, plus other small things for success.

Elizabeth had her piano teacher playing when everyone came back to the house. Their yard manager, Henry, had flowers everywhere!

Ruth had insisted it be a small ceremony, but that was one wish she didn't get for when anyone heard of the match and the upcoming nuptials they made mention of coming or helping or some such that led to adding on the original guest list. Her parents would be all right with it when they saw how happy everyone was to be included and the good will that prevailed. A special surprise was that General Haden and a number of the officers who had served in France were also coming unexpectedly. How great was that! Their minister was to perform the service and he was pleased and honored that the military would come..

Ellie hurried upstairs to see how the bride was doing. Ruth's personal maid, hired by Alfred was fitting her into the gorgeous wedding gown. My darling daughter I cannot believe how very elegant this is!"

"You deserve to be a most beautiful bride, although you would be in even a sack, you are indeed breathtaking now."

"Flattery is it, Miss? I cannot believe we are having such a huge affair when all I expected was a little quiet ceremony and a dinner here."

"Oh, but Mama, everyone loves you and as a result have come to love father as well. It is what you both deserve and I am so very glad to have a hand in it! Lady Jane sent a message and all is ready at the church so I do not need to run like crazy to and fro. We have had word that ten more local people are coming and the church is so full additional chairs have been placed in the vestibule. Father will enter from the back with the minister and a small pathway has been made for your entrance. I had never heard of people coming to a wedding without an invitation but it just shows how much everyone loves you both. Do not tell father (oh, well you won't see him until the ceremony so I guess you can't.) but a whole group of his regiment are coming. I knew a few days ago and they have been given comfortable chairs in the front – some being still infirm from the war. They have spent the night at General McPark's estate and will travel in a parade of carriages that the General arranged. It includes enlisted men, a couple sergeants, and some officers. This is in addition to the officers that General Haden is bringing.

Here I have put four extra handkerchiefs in your reticule, because you may both cry. Do not worry about the food, Lord Edward and Lady Dierdre Morton have arranged for much more than we planned and assure me that there will be sufficient with extra to be passed out to the needy, which of course was my suggestion. They sent staff with it and it arrived an hour ago – a wagon full - and with the instructions their people are to remain to assist with serving. Evidently Lady Dierdre Morton is just as efficient and helpful as her sister-in-law. The two children will be here at the house with their nannies and should arrive momentarily. One is Lord

Edwards' and of course the other is Jane's – or I beg pardon – Lady Baden's."

"How in the world did Henry manage all the flowers, Dear. He has not been so well of late. I hope it wasn't too much trouble."

"Oh, not to worry. Mary and her husband, that handsome sheriff, came from Summerwood and are in charge of the flowers and all is finished. They even brought added vases and urns, loaned by Lady Jane. Mary is expecting her first child so I provided them the blue bedroom for last night and tonight, so she would not have to travel if tired after all the partying. Mary also has your bouquet made and will give it to you as you enter the vestibule at church."

"My darling Elizabeth, you have absolutely thought of everything. Thank you so much! And to have members of Alfred's regiment…how thoughtful of you and of course will be such a great pleasure for my husband.

One other question, my dear daughter, how am I to ever get all this skirt into the carriage?"

"Well, it will be interesting but Julie is coming with us and between the three of us holding it up we should be fine. Thankfully there has been no rain and the path should not be muddy. I will hold on one side, Julie on the other and you will not yet have your bouquet so you can hold the front and we can easily miss the fence catching it or anything happening amiss. Are you certain everything is comfortable? Is your hair as you would wish?"

"It is all perfect. I am so very excited. I have loved Alfred so long and this is just as it should be. Thank you, Daughter, for your love and of course your help. It is amazing what a few women can do when romantically inclined." Laughing she hugged her.

Elizabeth hurried and slipped her gown over her head with some help buttoning from Julie and the ladies were ready to proceed to the church. Her father had gone sometime early that morning, hoping to visit with some of the guests, including officers before things got too hectic to do so. He would be thrilled when he saw even more of his military comrades.

As they got to the pretty country church, the carriage driver assisted each lady to exit and helped straighten skirts, crinolines and so forth. Mary was at the church door holding Ruth's bouquet just as planned. There was a very, very full church. Elizabeth noticed several rows of men, some in uniform and some bandaged or missing limbs seated in several rows at the front of the church. Elizabeth tried hard not to cry but a tear rolled down her face. Her Dad was going to be so proud! Lady Baden had flowers and lighted candles in each of the church windows.

As they had all skirts straight and Ruth took the bouquet from Mary, Doctor Ormond took Ruth's arm as planned and Elizabeth started down the aisle in front of them on the arm of Kenneth Thompson, who had been asked by Ruth to be Elizabeth's escort. Elizabeth managed to smile as she headed down the aisle toward her father in time to the procession. That man looked so proud and was smiling more than she could ever remember him doing. She took her place with Ruth beside Alfred, in front of the minister.

Elizabeth was most happy looking at the couple exchanging vows! The Reverend gave the ending prayer, thanking God for Alfred's healing and the love of the two now wed. Then he asked for all to provide good faith and support for the couple and please go to the estate for refreshments.

The church organ began what Elizabeth assumed was the wedding march or recession and she with Kenneth followed her parents out of the church. It was so nice to think of Ruth as her mother now. No disrespect for her poor deceased Mother but she could not love Ruth any more than if she had given birth to her. She was to ride back in the Thompson carriage to give privacy to her parents and she blushed as Lady Thompson told her how beautiful she looked .

It was doubtful that any in the village had ever seen such a great accumulation of carriages and gentlemen on horseback as went through the town toward the Glass Castle.

Arriving back, the entire wedding party and guests were greeted by Henry, Jim and three other men who were in dark suits and helping with horses and carriages. Wendell Bates, the deputy who lives on the Baden estate, was resplendent in his uniform and doing door duty. Giving his big grin and lovely manners a show to all.

The wedding couple received a sounding round of applause as they stepped out of their carriage, Kenneth moving quickly forward to assist at Alfred's elbow without making a show of it.

The Major greeted the men from the army hospital and then his fellow army officers. Thanking both Generals for bringing them. What a joy that was to see him laugh and tease and reminisce! It was all a surprise for him, although he had been writing to them for some time.

As soon as most everyone had entered, the same sheriff was being used as a climbing pole by the children present. He gently but firmly had them follow him to the study where a special banquet was prepared just for them with frosted hand cakes and sandwiches…much to their liking because they could use their fingers.

Many comments were made about the lovely music coming from the pianoforte and the teacher was making very nice selections. Lively and pretty but not so loud people couldn't talk and visit.

Tables were set up in every nook and cranny and even a number on the patio outside. Food had been ready exactly on time and the bridal couple cut the cake and fed each other and everything was happy and successful. Elizabeth noticed Dierdre Morton sketching and thought it was for a portrait of the wedding couple as she had promised. Elizabeth made certain to go to each helper, the military enlisted men and officers, and the ladies such as Kenneth's mother, Jane, Dierdre, and the piano teacher and thanked them again.

Elizabeth didn't worry about food because the Mortons supplied enough extra that nothing was scarce. Lastly the tall, beautiful wedding cake was cut by Ruth and Alfred with two other cakes cut by staff. It was the best of parties. Lady Edward Morton (Dierdre) came to her and said they had one hundred and ten people, if the counting was correct. The largest congregation, according to the wife of the minister ever in their church.

By evening the throng had pretty nearly disbursed, Elizabeth making certain proper dishes were returned to Dierdre and any others including some to Jane. The military gentlemen were escorted to their carriages amongst much clapping and many had packages of food or cake to take along as ordered by Elizabeth and overseen by Sarah from the kitchen. Alfred, who had been seated to rest his leg, stood at attention and saluted as they left and there was hardly a dry eye in the house. Most returned the salute if not incapacitated and Elizabeth thought she would never, ever forget the scene! Carriages for the Morton and Baden families had pulled out, after the children had bowed and properly thanked Elizabeth, Alfred and Ruth for the "party". Elizabeth had packaged up cake for them to take home.

She insisted Mary sit in a comfortable chair and rest for she had been on her feet too long for an expectant mother. She offered to do some clean up but was told absolutely not and her husband came and lovingly kissed her head and told her to rest all was satisfactorily finished.

When things were finally all in the kitchen or other proper places, Elizabeth sat down heavily into a comfortable chair, realizing she should not have done so because she may not be able to rise again to go to bed! She watched as Big Jim, Henry, young Tom, Mary's deputy, Kenneth Thompson, and two others went to tour the property to be certain in the commotion no ner'do'well was left to cause any trouble. She heard her stomach rumble and realized she had not eaten a thing since breaking her fast that morning except the one biscuit she had grabbed. Well, she was too tired to worry about it now. Just then Kenneth came up with a plate for her and a small table. He said he had noticed she did not take time to eat. All was well outside. He was a keeper although unfortunate too old for her, at least yet!

They talked while she ate and both said they were surprised and quite pleased that the whole huge thing had come off without any problems, no carriages threw a wheel, nothing of consequence was spilled, all the poor souls from the army seemed fine and the day was a rousing success! The piano teacher had left escorted by her husband and Elizabeth had reached to pay her but she refused any recompense and said it was her great pleasure to be part of such a wonderful occasion and that the army men's enjoyment of the music was more than pay enough. Elizabeth wrote herself a note to see what was involved in her providing a piano and player for the army hospitals.

Her father came over limping more than usual but assuring her he was just fine. Kenneth said he had been invited by Ruth to stay the night and had let his parents know. As Kenneth took her dishes to the kitchen, she realized she loved him...well, how about that as young as she was – she wouldn't tell!

The next morning, after a delightful sleep, hearty breakfast and short ride over a couple fields, Kenneth kissed her on the forehead and left. She felt her heart leave with him. When had THAT happened? Well, over time she guessed but he was wonderful!

144

CHAPTER ELEVEN

Now was the start of Ellie being more of an adult and less of a child. Her fifteenth birthday was here but there was not to be a party. They did have a dinner for Kenneth and his family, the Badens, the Mortons, and a few of her parent's friends but much more quiet than the wedding! Thankfully!!

Lady Baden took her aside and asked her about things Ellie had thought of doing to the estate, saying she had heard something about a school.. Evidently, Ruth had given away about her idea of helping indigent children or others who wished to better themselves without much encouragement from elsewhere. Lady Jane said please tell her what she planned for her school. Briefly Elizabeth explained what she hoped and got rousing encouragement from Lady Jane with offers of help..

While they were talking she would like to know about the lovely floral arrangements on the porch. It was her understanding that Ellie had designed them? Well, no, said Ellie. She had seen the like in London almost seven years ago, had Henry duplicate them and they took the time needed to always have them look nice. She suggested she help Jane make some too and the two agreed to get together to do so. Next spring, she hoped to do more of them in the yard near the drive, the spare building where her school would be and at the back door.

She really enjoyed talking with the lovely, petite Lady Baden and felt she was a friend to them all.

The more Ellie thought of her classes for her "school" the more she felt some about farming and orchard study would be helpful to any who wished to work on or run a farm. Maybe even flowers for sale would be a nice addition to some properties and help the families financially. She would talk to father, James and others but really felt those classes should be added. Oh my, this was turning into a huge process. Jane assured her it all sounded quite nice and to not be discouraged at all the work it would entail.

For the next year Elizabeth compiled ledger after ledger of what was needed in order to start her school for others less fortunate. She, now sixteen, had permission from Ruth and her Father, to use the big stone barn as the principal schoolhouse and staff removed any remnants of animals or stalls – a good choice because a couple years before her death, her mother, Madeline, had seen to constructing a more modern and larger barn closer to the fields and this one was virtually vacant. Really it was <u>her</u> barn, but she felt it polite to get her parents' approval, after all the commotion of the whole process would infringe heavily on everyone living in the Glass Castle.

146

Ellie (now really Elizabeth) was growing like a weed and another shopping trip was arranged to buy further dresses for she grew a couple inches a year and the nice ones purchased over two years ago were already looking small. Although Henrietta, an additional maid hired to help with hair, clothes and so forth, had added panels, lace and other means to make the nicer ones still wearable.

Elizabeth was now taller than Ruth and starting to look more like a woman than a girl. Her increased height and serious manner showed she was really grown up. Alfred and Ruth found she had finalized her Glass Castle school plans with little change needed and was a most serious student having progressed in her lesson work much faster than the normal school sessions would have done.

She wondered if Kenneth would like her new dresses. Encouraging Ruth to also get new clothes, Ellie was excited to see Ruth model them when they got home. "Oh, Mama Ruth, how beautiful you look!" Ruth grinned at her and assured her she did like hers very well. "I am so very pleased you agreed to get some new outfits too."

They did a fashion show for her father. Holding the door wide for her, Ruth stood back and Elizabeth entered. The two of them had put her hair up on top of her head with the new combs given by the store, and this dress in a medium blue with white lace and some pink flower embroidery on the bodice fit her slim figure to perfection. She stepped through the doorway and bowed to Alfred. Well, good heavens, the man almost cried! He quickly coughed to get his composure and raised himself up higher on the settee.

"Oh, my, I have always known you were beautiful but not that you were a beautiful grown woman! Oh, my darling girl! Well, you are indeed lovely. The blue is exactly like your eyes and you look so very tall and mature!" Both would remember how his eyes lit up at their appearance – forever!

Growing up entailed less enjoyable things than shopping, however. Like public appearances and advanced school. She liked the school and classes well enough but the boys always bothered her. When she complained to Ruth, it was explained that young men, as they were indeed, found it hard to get the attention of girls they liked without acting silly and that as they matured she would probably like them better. Well, tarnation, would she? Yes, maybe so, she already liked Kenneth Thompson very well, her only complaint being he had not in the past taken her idea of a school for the less fortunate as seriously as she. And being older he was not like the gauche young men she had encountered at school.

A couple years ago, he had said it was foolish to spend such money on the likes of store clerks and farm hands. That quite upset her and although she continued talking with him and would allow him to sit by her in church, she was having second thoughts about him being any kind of permanent beau – although she was afraid she was indeed falling in love with him! She didn't know that his opinion had changed, however. She was soon to find out just how much.

———

Elizabeth had progressed well with the plans for a school at the Glass Castle. Her dream since early childhood! She had outlined much of what she needed and discussed it often with her parents and others: including the Badens, the Thompsons, Dr. Ormond, the Richardsons, the Randolphs, Lord Henry Morton, the Moores and any number of others. It would take a year to refit buildings and actually start such an endeavor – but she would prevail! She knew she was ready to start now.

All this activity, shopping, performing in a piano recital, and harder classes came as she was growing into a lovely young lady, with the dignity of a grownup. Now she was to play the piano in public. She fervently hoped this was the last of these public displays, but realized she was not as frightened

149

anymore as she had been during the spelling bee. And horrors, the Thompsons walked in…well, if that wasn't enough to scare her nothing was! Just before she was to perform Kenneth presented her with a corsage. Well, tarnation she almost cried.

Her performance was flawless and she was very relieved but assured her teacher she would not do so again. Explaining that her school she was creating would take up any practice time she had.

The next few weeks were tests, and more tests, which reluctantly she attended and succeeded remarkable well. Her reluctance was not from disliking the subjects or any effort required but just the time it took from her creating her own school for others! Finally, she had passed everything with remarkable grades and it was over. She had graduated two years ahead of most and was finally able to concentrate on HER ideas and all the changes to the Glass Castle estate it would take.

Alfred did not want her restricted to the estate as his late wife had been but worried about her beauty and wealth being a catalyst for unwanted attentions. However, Ruth explained they could not keep her forever at the estate and both had talked to her extensively on taking care with whom she made friends and calculating who could and could not be trusted. Her bodyguard, William may have seemed odd to some people, but they didn't know her great wealth and her parents were afraid some 'ner'do'well just might!

Cautioning her until she was ragged with the need to keep her wealth a secret and just let people believe the only income she had was from the estate for rentals, cattle and produce. Many would know there must be more income for such a huge estate but would not probably know about the other advantages such as the industries and other farms. She was assured by her parents, no one need to know that she had drawers full of investments, cash and stocks – handled by her original attorneys and now two more. Typical parenting problems arose continually being new to both Alfred and Ruth. But since they were in good accord on how to handle things it made them closer rather than separating their affection. Elizabeth was always accompanied, as mutually agreed.

She was now old enough to attend well chaperoned teas and concerts and bring friends home for riding or dinner. In return she was invited to many such events as well but thankfully also with her father, Ruth, both or a chaperone. Kenneth Thompson was often in attendance also…sometimes the oldest one there but Ruth and Alfred understood his attention even if Elizabeth did not!

Alfred watched her and thought oh dear, how scary it was. His daughter grown up. And such a beauty and incredibly smart, too. At first he had wondered about her wanting to manage a school but was seeing it now as a good and generous idea. Plus, he was amazed, when encouraging her to share the things she had planned – she knew the costs, the building preparation, the books, the timing, the work schedule, teachers – she had it all planned out to the last detail. He knew she was unusually intelligent but was finding she was so organized with all things as well – quite an impressive combination. He hoped that any gentleman she liked would honor her in those ways as well as noticing her other attributes.

It certainly appeared the Thompson boy was attentive. Well, she could do worse.

CHAPTER TWELVE

Ellie was finished with formal schooling - very much to her unending gratitude and surprise – the time had gone quickly. Most of her classes had been college preparatory and therefore contained mostly boys with only a couple girls because the subjects were harder and more advanced and girls did not go on to universities. She had stayed with schooling, knowing the fortune she would need to eventually manage and also the complicated school she was about to start for others would require her to be as knowledgeable as possible. She felt the more education she could get while young, the better.

A dressmaker came to the house periodically over this time and fashioned some pretty but much less formal attire for her days at her school buildings and overseeing construction and improvements. She was now almost as tall as her father – outdistancing Ruth by several inches.

One extravagance: she had ordered at Ruth's suggestion, new riding attire and particularly liking a black riding jacket with buff riding skirt. In honor of these new clothes Ruth also bought her a black tall hat and she did indeed look like a grand woman when astride her new black stallion, also purchased from the stable near Essex recommended by Lord

Jonathan Baden, the husband of Lady Jane, her close associate.

Over these several years things had improved at the Glass Castle, a lot because of Ellie's insistence. Staff were increased where needed, compensated well, and had detailed work schedules. The estate was efficiently run and Ellie, upon encouragement, was handling many of the issues - and quite well too. She had been an exceptional student and had learned languages, as well as all normal curriculums but what she applied most were mathematics and business organization.

She had progressed to keeping a more detailed journal and mathematical listing of what she wanted to do on the estate. Mostly a means to run a free school for indigent children or untrained adults, who displayed an interest in learning and had no opportunities because of their lot in life.

Elizabeth was continually adding or changing her list of things to be taught and what was needed in teachers and supplies. She knew any type of addition, subtraction and calculation of things was vital. Also, good English grammar, which separated the educated from those who had not been. Some general information regarding geography and science too would broaden the students' perspective. She wondered often if it was taking on too much to also have a school of sorts for things like farm and crop management and animal care. She thought it a good idea. Certainly, some would get jobs that way and if possible maybe have small farms of their own at some point not only for revenue but home health for better feeding their families. She would talk with Father some more and maybe that nice Lord Baden or his smart wife, Jane, about that. She developed a whole curriculum for farming students so they would understand things like fertilizer, temperature change effects, bugs and tree or plant diseases. She felt certain she would do so…these people needed to be informed too and could attend only certain days to not mess up their current work schedules.

She energetically begun changing the estate to accommodate such a school. Her efforts had already made the big old building (the former barn) suitable for varying classes with just some furnishings to be bought. Now she was having a dormitory constructed for students who did not have daily transport. She had mentioned her intentions to both Father and Ruth and was afraid of some displeasure but wonder of wonders they both thought it all a marvelous idea! It was HER property they said and she should follow her desires – which they thought were quite honorable. They knew many might wonder about the high costs but of course, with her assets it was not a problem – such information though to not be shared.

She, even with her complicated plans, tried to do some music or horseback riding – sometimes now with her father, often also including Ruth, and of course Kenneth, kept her busy. Nothing was as important to her, however, as gathering information right and left for the furtherance of her estate goals. She had frequently corresponded with Lady Jane Baden and always got encouragement to follow her dreams and instincts and getting help and offers of any more she may need.

She was quite popular and invited to many parties and other outings – attending as she wished or had time but not shy about refusing when her schedule would not permit the time. Many boys asked her places but she refused. Father had some misgivings but Ruth would laugh at him and assured a chaperone would be in attendance should she ever accept such invitations. However, Ruth realized the girl only really liked Kenneth. She made certain Elizabeth had her pretty things, this was by far the most grown-up dressing Ellie had ever owned but after all she was of an age to do so – dresses without high necks and with more embellishments than ever before..

She was heartened by the fact that Kenneth Thompson had made many changes to his attitude about her school and the education of those less fortunate. He was now taking quite an interest and offering ways he could help and providing good encouragement. She was so very pleased. He had always been the young man she liked the most but their differences on her "school" had caused her concern. Now it looked like he may be one of her greatest allies along with her parents and the Badens. He had begun coming and working any time he wasn't tied up with his final year of university studies.

Elizabeth was mature in her manner and was very accomplished on the piano-forte and with estate plans. Her father and Ruth were regularly amazed at her stamina to continue so many things and do them all so flawlessly. Her horseback riding was very skilled and she could speed over the estate, jumping fences and hedgerows and leading any accompanying staff or guests on a merry chase. A couple times boys that were the sons of friends of Alfred or neighbors, were invited and one girl, a Thompson – cousin to the boy who visited most often was also adept at riding. They would make a fun day of it and then come back to the house breathless and very hungry, which made the kitchen staff happy. Staff would provide a meal complete with desserts. Finally, a party was arranged to include horseback riding, each invitee to bring their own mount and have a day of contests and an obstacle course. Jim and staff enjoying setting up the jumps and trials. It was attended by every person invited, all young men and women now. Everyone said it was the most fun they had enjoyed in a long time and over the scrumptious nuncheon provided by staff a lot of discussion was given to their futures. Elizabeth explained her ideas for the current estate as a school for the indigent. She was particularly pleased at Kenneth's interest and support – quite different than his opinion years passed!

Many of those attending were amazed that she would do so and would be allowed to open the estate to those less fortunate but on explanation admired her all the more. Kenneth realized the advantages of her "school" and would state it emphatically on occasion. He was adept at explaining to the others all the resulting advantages of such education.

She continued, when she could make a minute, interest in the beautification of the estate and had added floral arrangements in addition to the front porch and conservatory doors, many other places as well. She supervised the planting of flowering trees and shrubs throughout the property, including along the drive. She encouraged the hiring of a full-time gardener to take some pressure off of Henry and then added two assistants to the team as well. Next was creating two very large orchards of fruit trees to replace the old ones which had been planted most likely by the grandfather of Ellie's mother. These were helpful in providing food for the estate and school too. In all her busy schedule, she managed to spend two days with Lady Jane Baden and assist her in planting flowers and putting potted plants at varying locations at Summerwood. Also including a list of decorative and fruit trees that would be nice to add – which Lord Jonathan Baden immediately ordered done in addition to orchards he already had.

True to her financially conservative upbringing, she made certain that the cost of her improvements did not go beyond her budgeted expenditures…with additional income being made from the sale of increased farm products, fruits, animals and so forth not to mention the huge amount of interest earned on such good and abundant investments. With wise management she was increasing her wealth even with the school and plant spending. The Major was astounded at how well she kept the books and records of her endeavors and the money she was putting aside for the school and lodging for the less fortunate – her ultimate goal.

Ruth never called her Ellie anymore, for she was so mature. She was beginning to get a nice figure and she was a lovely and composed!

Elizabeth, like her father, was going to be unusually tall for a woman and she was quite beautiful. Both the Major and Ruth realized that she was often accompanied by or seen talking with the Moore or Richardson boys as well as Kenneth Thompson and although chaperoned always, they didn't seem to mind, which only showed that they were truly interested in her and her welfare. She realized her parents noticed her friends but didn't share with them her strong feelings for Kenneth.

Elizabeth had liked Mistress Edith Warren quite well. She and her husband - Robert, another Major had come to visit Alfred and they were so very personable, it was hoped they would visit again soon. Robert credited his life to Major Masters, saying he was injured and the Major had actually laid on top of him during a stampede caused by the French to drive them out of a thicket. Neither being run over but it was close and the important part was that he was willing to give his life if necessary for his men.
They promised to return and to bring their son and daughter. She guessed she would interest them with horseback riding, borrowing her parents' horses and a couple from Jim. That would be a start, that's what she talked to the others about and she really, in all honesty wasn't interested in attracting the interest of any except, of course, Kenneth. She decided to invite Kenneth as well. She didn't discuss her affections, being still a little shy about it, but it would take a most impressive boy to draw her interest away from him. Hesitant a long time ago, Kenneth now was a support for indigent schooling and was making suggestions and offering assistance every time she turned around, not to mention frequently helping staff with the new building or refitting the old barn.

160

She was certain she had persuaded him to like the idea, why else would he be such a help?

He had even discussed things with her father that might be good additions and had promised his work and to procure some of the supplies needed. Fancy that.

Well, tarnation! She had been daydreaming and needed to get to the construction of the new building at the back of the old barn. The new building would be a dormitory, housing students who did not have means to travel regularly and would provide sleeping and eating accommodations and a separate wash house with showers and privy holes of their own. She hurried out the back door.

Kenneth was being very encouraging.. He had come several times recently and worked with four of his staff, helping do all kinds of things, even dirty construction and glazing windows. As her father would say: "He is a keeper!" She worried about the time it was taking him away from his university studies – although she knew from friends his grades were exemplary.

She hated that he may be in university awhile yet this year because they didn't see each other very often when he had school. Being brilliant like his father, he would finish Eaton two years early however, and already had a position with Parliament promised as part of a legal research team. He hoped to test for his juris prudence degree at the end of graduation.

Today as she walked up he was right there at the new dormitory. She explained she could have staff move some of the stored school furnishings into the main area of the old barn building now and the upper floor was ready for beds, a closet and two dressers. With his help and good staff, it was coming along very well. He told her to be certain to write or send a rider so he would know when to come and help again as she needed. He would bring two of his father's men also. They worked together, supervising three men but also doing considerable labor. Finally, he said he had to be going but would see her soon. She grinned her dimpled grin as he kissed her hand, quickly giving him a peck on the cheek and making him blush. She watched him leave to get his mount and head for home.

She almost jumped out of her skin when her father said, "A really fine young man you have there, Elizabeth. I approve of him wholeheartedly! Your mother and I want to thank you again for the lovely wedding anniversary party you gave us last week. We cannot believe the number of people, three dozen, and all the plans it must have taken when you are so busy with your school. It was superb and we are most thankful, dearest heart."

"Oh, Father you do not need to keep mentioning that it is past and it was my pleasure. So nice seeing the neighbors. Here take a look at the upstairs, if your leg feels well enough....Kenneth helped us and the bedrooms are almost finished except for a few more furnishings. We just need to add mattresses, bedding, slop jugs, wash basins and pitchers, oh, also desks with oil lamps so they can study if they wish.

On the first floor will be tables with benches for studying and eating their meals, a small kitchen area, a long table for serving food and a really large wood stove for heating the whole building. Staff had added a large pot for heating tea water, and a set of small canisters for tea and sugar. Their contribution they had told her."

Again, her parents marveled at her organization.

CHAPTER THIRTEEN

Elizabeth reflected on how much more she had to do to the upstairs classrooms, in the refitted barn building where the more accomplished students would be taught with the younger and less learned downstairs. For two days she had not been out to the school with several estate issues and a visit to the lawyer which took up almost a day with the ride to and from London. She need slates, bookcases, tables and benches and so forth.

She had just finished writing to Kenneth Thompson as an extra thank you for not only dormitory building help but for his encouragement and great assistance in general for her school for the indigent. She also wished him well with the testing he would face. He had been stalwart in his help and advice, not hesitating to get his hands dirty, or bringing supplies without reimbursement. Taking time from his studies or coming after a day in classes. He was a good man...not a boy anymore, but a good man!

She was aware how popular he was and that a number of classic beauties, more his age, were very interested in him. She worried about that a lot! She knew he had attended Almacks on occasion, although her informant said he rarely danced and never more than one with the same person.

Definitely sitting out the more formal dances later in each evening. Although many girls talked to him!

He spent a good bit of time with her, it wasn't a "date" in any stretch of the imagination. They had not "stepped out" together specifically – everyone thinking she was too young she supposed....but she knew she wasn't. Well, anyway it never hurt to receive a thank you note she thought as she wrote to him.

She was inundated with work on her school, she found out Father and Mother were planning a small dinner for her to celebrate her completion of school early, although it was a few weeks past. She assumed they would invite Kenneth but hadn't been consulted so she couldn't be sure. She had encouraged them to postpone the event until her school was finished but they just grinned and said it wasn't a big affair. Just some friends. If Kenneth wasn't invited and a number of the other boys who had shown some interest were, she was very concerned that the wrong impression may be given to any of those fellows involved...Kenneth included! She probably shouldn't even be worried...her chance of a regular beau was probably a while away but at least now she was officially months passed seventeen she would hope to be allowed to go places with her choice of boys – chaperoned of course! She knew she loved none other than Kenneth, with an abiding love, a real adult love.

165

She would be more than a year older than the age when Lady Jane Baden had realized she and her Jonathan were in love, or so Jane had secreted to Elizabeth. Well, she would try waiting a bit but she certainly wasn't very good at such.

This wasn't getting anything done. Balderdash! She had today's mail ready and would find Henry or someone to post it for her. She needed to go to her school building and see how the construction of rooms had progressed the last few days....so much to do. Oh, and ask Henry about the plantings around both the school and dormitory building. Staff had been asked to clean the place up and polish any floorboards, clean windows and reglaze several of the older ones that had cracks – the replacement glass having arrived the week before.

As she reached the reclaimed barn area, Elizabeth heard talking and something obviously very heavy being scraped along the floor and she hurried inside. She saw nothing, then realized the noise was above. As she went up the stairs, they were much less creaky and very sturdy now…someone had worked on them a lot. The handrails were smooth and sturdily supported too.

When her head was just above floor level she peeked to see what all the commotion was about and there were Big Jim, two men she didn't know and none other than Kenneth! They were installing a slate board for writing on one wall, already reinforced she noticed, and had a dozen of the desks with chairs attached just as she had wanted lined up facing it. She must have gasped, because the men turned and then laughed. "Well, so much for that surprise!" said Kenneth.

"What do you think, Miss?" asked Jim.
"I hardly know what to think – how wonderful you are. This is exactly as I had wished but did not have an inkling it was this near ready…my goodness, you must have worked like fiends!" She said, blushing profusely.
"Kenneth, how did you manage with school?"
"Well, I had the highest grade so did not have to take the final exams. I have been out of school for a week and working on this project of yours the whole time. I just saw to the bringing of the slate and brought the desks today in three carts. We had dismissed the men about an hour ago. I have my mount in the stable and decided I would help your staff with the installations."
Seeing him standing beside the very large Jim, Elizabeth was struck with the fact that although leaner, he was every bit as tall. Fancy that. He was all grown up.
"I don't want to spoil your surprise, but may I bring my parents to see this? Father is quite well today and I believe he could maneuver the staircase with a little

help." "We had hoped to have it complete with bookcases and maps but of course, why don't you go ask if they would like to come. I would love seeing the expressions on their faces when they see this is almost a reality now. My professor of geography at school is contributing several maps, he was so enthused about your project when I shared the news with him."

"Oh, how wonderful of him to be so understanding of my goal. Please give him my thanks and provide me his address so I can correspond later. I'll be right back."

Elizabeth hurried to the house and breathlessly rushed into the library. Mother was sitting at the piano, playing some cords and small tunes the piano teacher had given her – now she had been convinced by Alfred to take some lessons. Father was in the big chair and looking comfortable, she almost hesitated to bother them, but couldn't hold her excitement.

"All right, Darling Girl, what's up? I can see you are excited about something. Since you are not in riding clothes I take it that you didn't get the horse to do all the jumps, so what has you in a dither?"

"Oh Father, Mother, I hate to disturb you but can you come to the school for me a minute? Do you feel well enough Father to make the walk and then climb the stairs?"

168

"I do indeed, and it is good timing. We were reflecting just a bit ago that I had not walked enough today…it will be a good stretch for these old legs. Ruth, Dear, would you like to come too?"

"Oh, indeed I would, an excellent excuse to stop my bothering this piano. I'm very afraid I will never be very good. Let me grab a wrap."

"Well, I can see quite an improvement in the last few weeks of your piano playing and you can entertain me when we rest from the walk….let's go see what has Elizabeth so excited."

As he walked carefully over the uneven ground, Ruth realized that although they had staff make the paths to the barn and flower garden more level, they still needed to work on other places that her Dear Alfred might want to walk. But he used his cane and they took their time and arrived at the barn without accident.

Kenneth and Jim were there to greet them and invited them in the school first. Much had been done there, all clean and the floor repaired and polished. A stage built, they assumed for teaching a large group or some kind of performances or general instruction of the entire assemblage. There were many benches with comfortable backs, all looking brand new and polished before the stage…probably at least eight or more, with slim writing shelves attached to the back of each for the students behind to use for desks.

Motioning upstairs, Elizabeth put her hand to her father's back on the side with no arm and together they made good headway up the long flight to the second floor.

"Oh, my, Ruth Darling, would you look what they have done! And with help from you Kenneth Thompson? Why Boy, how have you had time?"

"Yes, Major, I have indeed and with great pleasure. I brought the wall-slates and some things this morning and have been working here this week to surprise Elizabeth. I think I succeeded, because she was speechless and we know that doesn't happen often!" He could barely get the last sentence out for laughing as Elizabeth hit his arm and laughed as well.

Jim spoke up: "The lads at the barn were so excited, realizing their siblings or children would have a means to schooling at hand that they have worked on their own time to make benches and bookcases for up here from boards out of the shed we pulled down last year, which we will finish bringing now the floors have been cleaned. Some are already as you can see, and some placed in the room below. They did an excellent job with a plane then sanding and polishing until they are smooth."

"Oh, I am so proud of you all and forever grateful for your help. This is beyond where I thought we would be in a couple months hence. You are so wonderful!" and Elizabeth sobbed much to her embarrassment.

"Well, it was your brilliance and good works that have done it, my darling daughter. Although I too am very pleased for all this help you have been given. Won't you fellows take a break now and come to the house for nuncheon? You too Jim. We would be most pleased and when we left the house the smells from the kitchen were indeed appetizing. Oh, and I see that John and Wendell are helping and I am including them of course."

The fellows not wanting to admit it but were quite hungry from their morning of work. That young swell was quite a fellow. He could do a day's work even if his clothes cost above theirs by a hundred! They wondered if he wasn't sweet on Miss Elizabeth but doubted he would indicate that until she turned eighteen…didn't do to make the father angry.

Big Jim was thinking much the same when he saw how Elizabeth blushed when she would look at Kenneth. And how often did a rich swell like this boy – well young man – work on their days off, getting dirty and tired and eating a cold sandwich out of a saddle bag. Well, if he was sweet on her and she obviously liked him, it was good….yup a good match. Both willing to work for a good cause despite their wealth and privilege. Not often found but really fine – for the both of them.

Jim couldn't know it but the Major was thinking along the same lines. His daughter was an exceptional young lady. Privileged beyond most any

171

other he knew but generous and kind. A school for heaven's sake…who would have thought it. But she was exactly correct…education separated the masses from those who lived comfortably, even when not royal. His own education had enabled him to achieve good rank in the military, although he had no royal blood…yes this was a rewarding project and made him very proud of his daughter.

After successfully getting her father down the barn stairs, Elizabeth relied on Ruth to get them to the house and she hurried ahead to alert the kitchen to a large nuncheon service. She would help them heat some extra vegetables and she knew they had baked bread and cakes that morning. They could fry some of the large ham from last night to go with the baked chickens and with lots of fruit for compote it would be a good nuncheon for everyone.

If staff thought it necessary they could fry some potatoes too. If she knew anything about food, she knew men loved fried potatoes – of course she did too. She would help peel – she had often done that as a lonesome child looking for something to do in a much too quiet household. Boy those days were gone for sure and certain…the place was a veritable Piccadilly Circus!

After staff hearing that such big men were expected Elizabeth did find herself peeling potatoes and then frying them in lard and watching then turning until they were nicely brown with crispy edges. Using the iron skillet that was two burners wide for the great amount of potatoes peeled. Staff smiled at each other, so proud of the young sprite – now almost a grown woman. She chopped some onions and after putting the browned potatoes in a huge bowl, browned the onions as well, knowing some men, including her father loved the browned onions.

She started to the dining room and almost dropped the huge bowl of potatoes, when Kenneth took them from her. She grinned – "the grin" – and then he almost dropped them!

He returned and then took a tray from Betty as well. She just shook her head in amazement and gave it to him never thinking to refuse, it surprised her so. My goodness that new fellow was certainly well brought up, but from his clothes he looked like he must be a swell....no one she knew could dress like that!

With all kitchen staff on board and Elizabeth and Kenneth carrying things to the dining room, nuncheon was soon ready. The major asked Elizabeth to say grace and she did without hesitation, including thanking the gentlemen for their hard work to improve the lives of many through the new school and paying homage to her parents.

Dishes were quickly passed and if the kitchen staff didn't think their food was appreciated they should have stood watch....for the men certainly did it justice. As they finished a lot of what was on the table, staff brought in two peach pies and a chocolate cake....chocolate no less...many did not get anything chocolate except maybe at Christmas – but a whole chocolate cake – well they could certainly help demolish that.

Letting the men eat all they wanted until they obviously were not going to take anything else, Alfred got a big piece of what was left of the chocolate cake and grinned at Elizabeth.

"Did you know it was my favorite? Or did I just get lucky?" He had a chocolate mustache and Elizabeth had to laugh at him. He looked like a giant guilty child!

"I guess I didn't know it was your favorite. Mother, did you know?"

Elizabeth had to laugh harder, for Ruth had a mouthful of chocolate too. "Well, at least I now know what your favorite dessert is."

Even their guests were grinning, many also with chocolate showing. Elizabeth graciously thanked them all – by speaking to each man in turn. "It is my dream but you have facilitated it and helped me so very much. I thank each and every one of you.

Kenneth, you have come a long way every day and helped on a project not your own, and I thank you from the bottom of my heart. I will never forget your unselfish contribution to my school."

"I can't speak for the others, but for me it was a great pleasure and I admire you more than words can say for your unselfish interest in bettering the many lives this school will touch. You are indeed a very special person." Said Kenneth with some gravel in his speech, showing he too was emotional about the school and the girl, of course.

All the gentlemen thanked them profusely for the delicious nuncheon and each went their respective ways, three back to work and Kenneth to the stable to get his horse for his ride home. As he parted he said he would be back in two days to help some more. It was probably too forward, but Elizabeth took his hand and squeezed it tightly telling him "thank you" again. She saw Ruth watching her but surprise, she wasn't looking askance or frowning but smiling and nodding her head.

Later inside, while Father was napping, Ruth came over to the piano where Elizabeth was playing and said she was so pleased at the progress on the school. How nice of the men and particularly Kenneth to give so much time and effort to her project. Elizabeth grinned and nodded. "Kenneth is such a good friend. I was very surprised at how much interest he has taken in the school and so many hours of work. Plus, he won't let me reimburse him for the slate and things…which are quite expensive."

"Do not be concerned about it. He would not have done it if he didn't want to. I imagine he is enjoying being involved and he obviously thinks very well of you and your efforts to get this school off the ground and successful. I have seen how he looks at you, and although he is somewhat older, I believe he cares for you a good bit."

"Oh, Mother, I so hope he does. I have cared for him for some time but felt I was not old or pretty enough to have his interest. I can hope but he deserves so much more than a young, not too pretty girl."

"What balderdash! You are beautiful. I realize you don't seem to know it but you are indeed. Plus, your many good works are much more important to such a serious and well brought up young man. He is a good person and will look for similar traits before he ever settles down. You provide those traits, do not sell yourself short, my Dear."

Elizabeth continued practicing her new music to help steady her mind and give her strength to finish her notes of what was needed, had been ordered and anything she might have missed for the school. With so much already done, she hoped to open it in a couple months or sooner. But Ruth's comments kept interrupting her thoughts. Oh, if only she was right. She had not done as much to the barracks and "quick" kitchen in the adjoining building so that would be her concentration now. She had ordered beds, pillows and mattresses. Thankfully, the roof was updated last year when she first planned this adventure so storage would not be a problem. The order for sheets, pillowcases and blankets was done already. Even a separate "out-house" had been built. She would also ask Jim to put a family of kittens into the barracks to protect it against bugs and mice or even rats. Jim and Timmy had found a great wood stove to use for cooking in the barracks and although it needed blacking, it was not cracked or seriously hurt in any manner. It had been left in an abandoned farmhouse, which had burned down a couple years ago and Lord Harmison, the owner of the adjoining estate was glad to get rid of it, planning to tear the remaining part of the burned building down. It had taken seven of their men to move it, but thankfully was now in the dormitory and getting its coat of "stove black". Having six lids to the firebox it would be large enough for what they needed and even had its own oven. Quite a find!

Oh Balderdash! She had forgotten to order the kitchen and eating area furniture…well that wouldn't take long. She quit playing and headed for the library where she had established a small office with a desk and drawered cabinet.

She quickly wrote out an order for the 4 long tables and 8 benches that would be the most she felt she would need. The order included a form for the seller to present to the Law Offices of the Right Honorable

Sir Edward Ambrose and Lord Justin Albert, for payment out of her "School Fund" – money she had set aside with them over a year ago, specifically for the construction and outfitting of the school for indigents.

She had been very honoured that both attorneys had contributed impressive amounts of gold to the fund to aid her school. Although they knew she, herself, could fund it – by adding their name to the contributors it gave credibility to the project and encouraged support by members of Parliament and other important people.

Having staff send off the order by post, she sighed and decided to change into her riding outfit and get some fresh air. She had eaten way too much at nuncheon and some exercise was needed.

As she changed she decided to see if her father was now awake from his nap and if both her parents would like to ride as well.

Hearing Ruth talking down the hall, she knocked on the door and sure and certain they were getting dressed in riding outfits. She laughed and explained that all three minds were of a same idea and could she join them or was theirs a private ride? They laughed at her and said of course she could come along.

Watching her father, she was struck again, as she had been many times lately, how much he doted on Ruth and how close they were….just perfect – absolutely perfect!

As they walked to the barn, Elizabeth suddenly turned to her mother. "Oh, dear, I forgot a couple things: I need Henry to order plantings and assign someone to be in charge of keeping the two buildings' grass trimmed – which I'm certain horses can do but also purchase some bushes and flowers. It will be much more appealing if looking trimmed and welcoming. Hitching rails can be put up for day riders' horses and keep them from eating any flowers. Jamie Pike can also see to proper hitching and barn access if the weather is unpleasant. Most will live in the barracks and not have an animal to ride, but I was hoping and expecting some commuting students from area properties too.

"My goodness, Daughter, does your mind never shut down. I am amazed how you have all this figured out."

"Well, I have planned this since I was about eight, before Mother passed. so have had a great deal of time to formulate what is needed, Father. And please if you think of anything, you will let me know?"

"Yes, child, I will let you know." And he chuckled, squeezing Ruth's hand.

CHAPTER FOURTEEN

For the next few weeks, people on the estate only saw Elizabeth for fleeting minutes as she hurried from barn to house, to school, to dormitory, to house, to barn and so forth. She had noticeably lost weight, which she didn't have to lose, and it took at least two servants of various expertise to accompany her on one errand or another. The bright spot was that Kenneth Thompson was much in evidence! It appeared he couldn't keep up with her either but he managed to work a good bit on the school building and on the dormitory – even much to her embarrassment helping finish the construction on the outhouse. He assured her he was keeping up with his law office work and made room on his calendar for this project too.

Every so often he would reel her in and make her take nuncheon or supper with him – the child would probably not have eaten at all but for that.

It was a huge project and word had gotten around the area and many of their friends, Alfred's military cohorts, and some of Kenneth's friends and relatives brought books, boxes of pens, even an abacus. Some also brought bottles of ink, more bedding, towels, many kerosene lamps, and four carriage-style lamps with metal shields to keep the heat from the wooden walls near the stairs where they were attached.

Likewise, some serving dishes and pans for the dormitory. Lady Jane Baden was not the least of the visitors, of course, bringing her son, helpers and always something nice – like schoolbooks, slates and jugs of ink. The cats had met Jane's son before and did not run, little Henry being taught the proper way to handle them and offering them pieces of his weathered looking meat and bread.

One day a very fine carriage with two out riders arrived and it was the friend of the Thompson's Lord Edwin Richardson, the father of the Lord Richardson who had been instrumental in helping Jane's brother, Lord Edward Morton, with the troubles regarding the illegal contraband. This Lord Richardson had also been one of the commanders in France so Alfred knew him at least by sight and reputation. It turned out he was a cousin of Kenneth's mother and so was most interested in hearing about the project and wondering if they had sufficient instructors.

When Elizabeth admitted she had not gotten the desired number yet, he stated that he was familiar with a similar school started by Lord Edward Saint James and Lord Henry Steele, with whom his son had gone to Eaton. Perhaps they would have some advice or extra maps or books…would she like him to inquire? He did not often get to see them for they were almost quarter of a hundred leagues away but he would correspond, if she wanted. He didn't want to interfere but would be glad to do anything he could to facilitate for her.

She thanked him profusely, assuring that such inquiry would be very welcome….she being completely new to this process. He agreed and then stated he would also be willing to teach – not regularly but on occasion, if they would put him up he could come for two or three days at a time and perhaps explain the military, combat, the need for such, plus grinning he said he was adept at maps and could teach anyone to read one.

Elizabeth was amazed and blushing said she would be more than honored if he would make himself available and also inquire for her. At that time her father came out and bowing to Lord Richardson invited him in for tea. As Kenneth came up the two men teased each other and Lord Richardson asked him what had precipitated him getting his outfit so dirty and yet why was he smiling so broadly. Could it be the young lady that was running the school? Elizabeth couldn't breathe. Oh, why had he done that! Then she realized that Kenneth had actually agreed with his relative and asked could he blame him. The elder simply said: "Not in the least!"

Well, this would be recorded in her diary tonight no matter how tired she was.

Conversation took up a lot of the afternoon, with suggestions from Lord Richardson as he toured both buildings. Including information and questions by him or the other way around by Elizabeth. He was obviously enthused and very complimentary. Often Kenneth would complement her as well and add some details of features she had included in the school or dormitory.

She answered many questions from their guest as to her interest in helping the unfortunate and how such a privileged girl had devoted so much of her time to such a very worthy cause – rather than gallivanting about in London with the Ton.

At first she had wondered if he was joking her but soon realized that not being the case but admiration at her devotion to helping the less fortunate and putting them in position to better care for their families and earn a better living.

Before they realized it, the evening shadows had fallen and it was dinner time and awfully late for their guest to travel a distance, being certain it would be quite dark before he reached his estate. Therefore, Ruth invited him and his two out-riders to stay the night and he graciously accepted.

Both Alfred and Ruth offered the chance for him and his men to freshen up for dinner, and Ruth being bowed to by Lord Richardson when she offered him and his escorts a rest before supper which would be in an hour.

Dinner was most enjoyable with Ruth and Alfred joining in the merriment. Everyone was struck with the pleasant person such a revered Lord could be when not fighting the French or ordering about at Parliament! Also, although she tried not to show it, Elizabeth was amazed at how the man could eat. No wonder he was as tall as his horse and muscled to boot. She wondered if maybe Kenneth would take after him - already being almost as tall but lean in his twenty-year-old build. She knew from the heat on her face she was blushing with such thoughts and immediately asked if they would like more dessert before retiring. Both Alfred and Edwin, as he had asked to be called, stated they believed they could indeed enjoy another brandy and some more of that fruit cake.

A week later, with things in very good shape for the opening of the school and dormitory, along came a huge parcel addressed to Mistress Elizabeth Masters. Inside were many books, some maps, and some large mathematical tables for hanging. A lovely letter from a Lord and Lady Edward Saint James was also enclosed. It seems they had been notified, by Lord Richardson, of her intent to form a school similar to one Lord Saint James had and they wished to be any help they could. They would visit sometime in the future but had just had their first child, a brother to his other three, so were staying close to home. Also, they too felt the need for more education to bring people up from a bad lot in life, they would be available for any help she would need – just write.

She flopped down on the stairs right where she had read the post and cried. That is where Kenneth Thompson, of all people, found her.

"Oh, Dear, what is the matter? Can I help you?"

"THAT is exactly the matter! Everyone is so nice, so helpful, I had thought I was alone in this except maybe for my parents and was frightened it would not work and I would put all these people to so much trouble and the others to false hopes – but it looks like it will work…and I am just overcome!"

"Well, Sweetheart, you are indeed going to succeed. It is marvelous what you have done and so many of us are as proud as peacocks with you. You have worked until you are thin as a rail and have to be tired to the bone but you keep on with your good ideas. You are a marvel – and I am here to tell you IT IS GOING TO WORK! Now suppose you show me what came in the mail that made you so upset. If you don't mind that is."

"Oh, I will gladly share with you, particularly with you, who have worked harder and longer than I, much to my great admiration and appreciation. Here read this letter and you will understand that I am overcome with so much help and good wishes."

While he read, she suddenly realized he had called her "Sweetheart!" now how in the world was she to look at him again without crying some more? Could he really mean it or was it just because he was trying to comfort her...oh, that he meant it. Oh, Lord, please have him mean it. I cannot possibly ever love anyone else...I have grown daily in my love for him as we worked together and I may only still be a girl, but I DO love him.

"I know who they are. She was his daughters teacher and attacked in a most vile way by a harridan of a woman who had wanted Lord Saint James attentions. She is a lovely person and they married after her recuperation from being thrown out a three-story window! Don't look at me like that it is true. We will go meet them sometime. They are both so very nice and they have a great school – not for as indigent as yours but similar."

"Why, goodness, isn't this lovely of them...and some really good books too. I don't believe but one is a duplicate of what you have either. Now, see how happy everyone is with you...how wonderful you are...attracting help from across the country. My uncle was very impressed and NOTHING impresses him." and he laughed. "I have a great favor to ask of you Elizabeth. I hope you will take it to heart."

"Yes, anything, Dear Kenneth."

"I wish you to rest today and tomorrow. Your birthday party is in three days and you are so worn out I am very afraid you will not enjoy it to the last second. I have checked the school and dormitory and there are only a very few things left on your list and Jim, your father and I will see to all of those. I came in to let you know according to your mother and father you are to rest, eat better than you have been, maybe ride a while this afternoon and just be a young lady for two more days. Can you do that for me?"

"I can, since you ask so nicely…yes, I can. But only if you will ride with me? I know you said you return home this evening, But can you take an hour to ride after nuncheon – I will rest until called to eat – I promise."

"Yes, that sounds perfect. You go rest and I will make one more tour with Jim and do a couple things I promised your father I would do. We will have nuncheon together and ride to the back woods this afternoon….then I must head for home, for I am not certain my parents remember me anymore." Laughing he waved as he went out the door.

As she lay across her bed with the cat purring beside her, she had a hard time turning her mind to rest and not rehashing everything. Spelling books – had she really seen the spelling books come? Yes they were on the fourth shelf. Math books, where had she put the mathematics books – they had come but where were they? Oh, in the tall cupboard Kenneth had built in the corner. Chalk, yes the chalk was there. Rest, I must rest, I promised I would rest. Petting the cat – now as big as her pillow, she let his gentle purr relax her and finally went to sleep.

Ruth and Alfred looked in her door and sighed. Finally! The girl had settled enough to actually go to sleep. Although they had not told her, they had often wakened when she would be up very early or even in the middle of the night, checking on things and checking on things. The poor girl – no longer a child – was so involved in this new school. It was indeed a wonderful thing and they had many neighbors inquiring about sending their workmen or a relative to the school. Some like town folk or families that did field work or ran small stores were absolutely thrilled that there would be a place of education for family members or workers and close at hand, too.

Of course, being a fairly new idea to educate the working class it met with opposition – some being afraid if you educated the help they would feel superior, but that was a small percent of the people....generally speaking it was consider a boon.

Two hours later Ruth, at Kenneth's urging peeked in Elizabeth's bedroom door. The cat had gotten up and exited as soon as the door was opened but Elizabeth still slept. She would give her another half hour and then wake her for nuncheon. The fellows, according to Alfred, had finished the last few items of the list and were in the stables looking over two new horses bought recently for staff. One of the older ones had gone lame and they allowed him to just meander and eat and live out his time as he wished. The second was just that they now needed another having hired an additional full-time man for yard work and errands.

It was this fellow that had planted around the school and dormitory. He knew flowers and plants it seemed and would be a great help now that Elizabeth had the property strewn with many flowering plants, decorative trees, fruit trees, and a vegetable garden to match none! Henry was aging and she needed to hire an additional person besides his two helpers, for he would not ignore an issue even to his detriment. No one would go hungry that was sure and certain. They had an abundance of robin's egg beans for drying and something called "sweet corn" like raised in the America's – an idea from Elizabeth of course and so very delicious. They believed Lord Baden had provided the seed. And to top it off, the new fellow said he would like to attend the school, never learning to read very well. How about that!

Shortly thereafter Ruth was reluctantly practicing her pianoforte and Alfred reading some war journals shared by Lord Richardson when Elizabeth appeared. She had changed into a riding outfit and redone her hair….looking quite the thing.

Grinning broadly, she said she felt like a new person and when would nuncheon be ready, for the first time in a while she was very hungry. Timing was perfect for at that moment Kenneth appeared and tapped on the door frame. "Did I hear someone mention nuncheon, I may waste away if I don't get invited to eat soon."

They all laughed and Alfred said he too was most ready for a meal. "Well, you men may want something to eat but as hungry as I am you may need to go to the kitchen for I have inspected the table and believe I can make a dent in the offering." said Elizabeth. Only then did she realize a "lady" didn't discuss hunger and such…oh well, she wasn't much of a lady anyway – hadn't she worked like a farm hand the last few months.

Kenneth pulled out her chair before staff could and she gave him her big grin. He was done! Cooked, signed and sealed, done! He had thought he was falling in love for the first time in his life but now he knew it and he couldn't be happier. His great uncle had teased him about it while here, and he had not denied the whole thing and he had to admit now that it was true.

He had graduated this past year and was ready now for a year internship with a good firm of attorneys. Then he would be ready to take a wife. However, he didn't know if she would be willing at just eighteen past at that time. He hoped so. It didn't matter where they lived. This being her estate, they could be quite happy here. For he liked her parents very much and all seemed in find accord.   He would practice law and could have an office here and only spend certain days in the city or maybe even open a rural office in addition.

With her school here, it made sense for her to remain. He suddenly realized he hadn't heard what someone was saying to him and jumped – laughing and saying he was miles away, which was only partly true. He had been asked to say the blessing and with pride did so immediately.

Alfred was watching him closely and realized everything that had passed between this young man and his daughter. It was obvious how they felt about each other. She was much younger than he would hope before she married and maybe had children, but it would be a fine match with Kenneth. He cared for her, it was obvious and he was well-mannered and educated. He would do. And she was quite mature.

After a delicious meal, including creamed potatoes, which Elizabeth said she had talked them into learning to make as a child, he asked about the cooking. He wanted instructions on the creamed potatoes, which he had never seen before. They were indeed tasty and he hoped to have them again sometime….maybe he could persuade the staff at home to make a similar dish. She told him she sometimes had staff add some grated cheese to them as well as the cream and that too was tasty.

191

She took his hand and led him to the kitchen, where a surprised Edna told him all about creamed potatoes and that the butter and flour must be well mixed before adding to the warm milk and potatoes or he would have flour lumps. He grinned, thanking her and said he believed he could impart the instructions properly.

Having eaten a hearty nuncheon and thanking staff profusely, they saddled up. Both were ready within minutes, for he had saddled his horse before Jim got hers finished. They rode like the wind! As they were approaching the woods, two of the men were loading logs and limbs onto a sled to be drug by the big dray horse. These were to be planed and used to build another garden shed beside the current one since considerably more food would be needed with meals being served to the day students (nuncheon) and three per day to the resident students.
Farm staff had already transported rocks from the fields where they had previously been stacked at the edges when clearing the land for easier planting. These would be the base for the new shed to prevent the wood from touching the soil and drawing moisture, which would soon rot it.

It was amazing how much work was involved in this whole process and how generous Elizabeth was with her inheritance to use it for such a good cause.

Kenneth did not know how wealthy she was but had understood from his family that her Mother had inherited a huge fortune and that the attorneys had invested it quite wisely to Elizabeth's benefit. It worried him somewhat that people may think he was after Elizabeth for her fortune. Nothing could be farther from his intent. In point of fact, he himself was quite wealthy anyway.

Well, that was a bridge to cross if or when they married but he certainly hoped no one would think that was what had attracted him to her. Just her good works and smile would be enough....no money needed!

When their refreshing ride was over, he kissed her on the forehead and bid her parents goodbye. She had tears in her eyes as he rode off, noticed by both Ruth and Father.

"We have not played the pianoforte together in a long time, Elizabeth. Do you have some time now...I play better when you are there to help me and add your excellent playing to cover my mistakes." Ruth laughed. Alfred took a comfortable seat on the settee to listen to the impromptu concert and was indeed impressed as his two loves played together. When they did a lovely Mozart piece, he was almost brought to tears. Tarnation! A Major crying over a piano piece, well he guessed so as he wiped his face and blew his nose.

CHAPTER FIFTEEN

Elizabeth's parents asked her was she ready to retire and she said not at all, her nap had been sufficient to give her more energy, and the ride with Kenneth had been short because of his need to get home for a while. Why had they asked? Ruth said they had thought about riding in the carriage to Ruth's house while it was still light enough to see the condition since the renters (or rather those she had loaned it to) had moved out the evening before.

They didn't expect it to be in any trouble, but would take an inventory with Ruth's butler and make note of anything needing to be done before fall set in. Elizabeth said she would love to go with them.

As they rode in the carriage, Ruth explained that she had hoped to make the house available for Mrs. Agness, the widow from the village whose house had sustained so much fire damage from a bad kitchen flue. The good widow was such a lovely person and would indeed take great care of the house and hers would need many months of repair before it was a comfortable and fresh place to live.

Elizabeth was so very pleased. What a great idea. The parents grinned at each other realizing their daughter had thought exactly as they wished. It didn't take long to make the trip and as they exited, the butler, Jeremy, came to the door.

"Why Miss Ruth, pardon me Mistress Masters, how lovely to see you. Come in and see how nicely the house has been taken care of. I hope you will be very pleased."

"Oh, Jeremy, I am so glad because I feel you will have a tenant very soon and it will get her a comfortable place quicker if we do not have to do a lot of improvements."

"Well, of course I can't say what you anticipate doing, but I know of nothing untoward. Everything is even clean. There are still some edible things in the cellar, like potatoes, onions and some crocks of pickles and so forth. Even some vegetables like carrots, herbs, turnips and parsnips. In the kitchen there are still some supplies as well. Several crocks of flour and sugar and even salt in abundance. And the place is spotless....your renters were very careful of the property and the Mistress Adams was immaculate in her handling of everything. They have left you a note and a little gift that I was going to bring to you in the morning but here, let me get it now."

Jeremy brought forth a small package wrapped in brown paper but with a pink ribbon and opening it with shaking hands, Ruth was amazed. Inside was the loveliest embroidered scarf, quite generous in length to go with a suit or coat or even as a decoration on a library table. The hand embroidery was exquisite and in nice pastel colors and quite intricate. "Oh, Jeremy, how lovely this is! She must have worked on it for many, many hours. I shall treasure it always."

"Well, they said you have been so very generous and kind to allow them to live here with no rent after their property burned. They knew they were in serious trouble, having no relatives to take them in and could not believe you would let them have your house rent-free."

"You know I do not need it, nor fortunately – thanks to Ellie's mother – do I need the rent it would bring. The logical thing was to allow someone to use it to keep the fires up and so forth. But where have they gone?"

"Oh, Mistress Adams has a brother whose wife is ill and they have made enough changes in their property to accommodate the couple and it will be a help to both."

Elizabeth noted how Aunt Ruth made it sound like they had done her a favor instead of the other way round. What a lovely person, how fortunate for her to have Aunt Ruth as a guardian for all the time her father had been gone. And now….well, now she was the catalyst that had gotten her father well and made him so very content too.

They did a quick turn around the house, looking in each clean bedroom, the private room was even clean and fresh. In the kitchen the stove had been newly blackened and everything was exactly as it should be…the dishes clean and in the cabinets and so forth. "My, my!" said the Major, "I don't believe you have to do a thing here, except order an additional couple cords of wood. How nice they have left it. Shall we stop by the widow Agness' house now and let her know to notify her son to get her moved post-haste?"

"Oh, yes, Alfred Dear, we can stop now before it gets any darker. Thank you so much Jeremy, will you continue to be the butler here and assist the widow with anything she needs? I will of course continue to pay you full salary and provide sufficiently with food and things for your comfort as well, if you care to stay."

"Why thank you so much ma'am. I will do so. I believe Mistress Agness has a maid who will come with her and that should be sufficient in this small a house. I will have much time on my hands and can keep up fires and so on for her."

"Well, all right then, it is settled. We will progress to the Agness house right now and get this finalized. Thank you so much Jeremy. I appreciate greatly how well you oversee the property for me. Good evening."

Back in the carriage Ruth asked Ellie to not forget for her to send Jeremy a "little something" for his extra trouble with the changing of tenants. She had not brought her reticule, never thinking things would be in such good condition.

Just minutes later they had drawn up to the Agness property. My it looked awful…windows blackened with soot and a hole in the back of the roof! It must not be very healthy for the widow to live there.

Hearing the carriage that very person came out with a heavy shawl around her shoulders. Smiling broadly.

"Why Mistress Masters, how nice of you to call and your husband and daughter, too. I have failed to send you my congratulations on your nuptials but I am so happy for you both. It is afraid I am to not be in much condition for company but Jimmy and I have cleaned the sitting room quite well and I have the tea kettle on the small stove in that room, come in, come in."

"Well, only for a minute, and there is no need for tea since I had left word I would be back home in time. I have some good news for you if you don't mind?"

"Well, looking around this place, I could certainly use some good. What is it, pray tell."

"You are familiar with my house just down the road and it is happy news that I tell you it is again vacant. We have just come from there and everything is in pristine condition. I would wish that you occupy it for whatever period you need – rent free. It would be to my great advantage to have a tenant so the fires are kept up and the place regularly cleaned. My butler will be there to assist you with anything and I will be paying him. Would you be interested?"

A minute later, Elizabeth worried that they may have to call the Doctor. For the widow Agness was beside herself with tears, and thanks, and more sobs. She called for her maid and Helen came immediately, looking slightly worn and her apron very soiled with soot.

"Oh, Mistress Agness, what is the trouble? Are you ill?"

"Oh, no child, I am not ill, just overcome with this lady's great offer." Helen looked at them inquiringly.

"Helen, dear, I don't know if you remember me but I am Ruth Roberts, now Mistress Masters, from down the street. I wish to let you and your mistress use my house and be certain it is clean and livable for as long as it takes to repair yours. Now it does not matter how long it takes – several years should be fine. There is no rent because you are doing me the great favor of keeping mine clean and warm and so forth.

My house butler, Jeremy, will remain to serve you and he has separate quarters in the back. He is a widower and quite clean and quiet. On occasion his two children may visit but they are grown up and no issue. He should present you no problems and will be considerable help in keeping up the fires, bringing up canned goods from the larder and so forth.

He can cook his own meals at a time convenient for you or join you if you care to invite him. The house has five bedrooms, one for each of you, the one in the back being for the same, Jeremy Anders, the butler who has had the room for a spell.. There is also an extra two should you have company or your son wish to spend a night with you. Oh, and there is a stable or sort on the property. In good repair, small, but maybe needing a sweeping out and it would need hay or feed added since it has not been used for several years or more. You will find Jeremy is even willing to do the walkways from dirt or snow and I feel you will find him congenial but very quiet and unassuming. He likes to read from my library there and you, of course, are welcome to do the same.

Will you do me the great honor of moving to my house to protect it and keep it from being empty and cold?"

"Oh, I would so love to do that. Are you certain you do not require rent?"

"No, no rent. Just the favor of keeping it clean and the fireplaces used. I don't know what food is left in the cellar or pantry but a few months ago there was considerable crocked goods and potatoes and so forth – please use anything like that so it doesn't spoil."

"I do need an answer if possible, for I will have to look elsewhere if you do not accept."

(Elizabeth tried not to grin at that – knowing while not a lie, it was more an encouragement to the widow Agness.)

"Well, I will say 'Yes!' certainly. I will send the neighbor boy to my son with this great news. He has been most worried about me, what with the smoke and all but has no room for me in his two-bedroom house and he now has two children. Will I need any furniture or things?"

"No just your and your maid's clothing or any personal items you would miss. There is a very comfortable rocking chair that I always liked in front of the fireplace and any number of other furnishings. I hope you find the bed comfortable. I had just purchased a new mattress prior to my going to Elizabeth's house when Madeline became ill so I didn't take mine with me…it has hardly been used. And it won't smell of fire. All linens and dishes and so forth should be available in the various cabinets and dressers."

"Mistress Masters, I am so very happy. May the Lord bless you for this generous offer. I thank you from the bottom of my heart." and the widow sobbed.

"Oh, I just thought, there will obviously be a lot of construction to fix the burn damage here….please feel free to transfer any of your things you want to protect to my house. There is an area in each

201

bedroom that would take something and a storage room behind the kitchen that has very little in it except some overly large pots and a very large iron skillet…that room would hold a goodly number of things too. As to clothes, please use any closet or drawer space you find except in Jeremy's room.

Here is the key and if there is a problem the butler should be able to help or you may send him to me for assistance."

Bidding her and the maid a good day, and aided by Alfred, they again took the road in their carriage – hopefully in time for tea.

"Mother Ruth, I think you missed your calling. You could have been a card player in the dens of London…you keep a great poker face on you when stretching the truth."

Alfred laughed so hard the driver looked back at them to be certain everything was all right.

"Well, Father, I do not exaggerate. You and I both know that Jeremy is perfectly capable of maintaining the property just fine. It is her good works that is afoot. She wanted to help the widow and made it turn around to where the widow thinks she's helping Mother. How clever! I will have to remember that tactic when trying to get my way."

"Oh, Lord help young Thompson. He will be dazzled and bamboozled all the time. Not that he isn't already…how many elite young men do you

202

know that would spend their entire vacation hammering and painting and so forth. Elizabeth you are quite a girl…you do me honor!" and he continued to laugh or snicker all the way to the Glass Castle.

She wasn't of age per her Mother's will, of course…twenty-one seemed a long way off. But she was old enough to have a chaperoned date, to make some decisions of her own, and she was finished with school last year so that too was behind her. Plus, her school for unfortunate youth was now ready to open in two weeks and she was more excited about that than almost anything.

Of course, she wouldn't say that to her dear parents. After much pestering of Ruth and her Father she managed to get an inkling of the guest list for her school opening celebration and was appalled. So many people! Well, she knew them all and really liked them all – at least somewhat. A couple of the young men could stay home as far as she was concerned. She enjoyed the jokes of some who would be welcome and of course wanted Kenneth Thompson's attendance above all else. In fact, if only Kenneth came it would be quite all right as much as he had helped he should be there! So many adults were on the list it was almost like an adult party.

She heard a great carriage pull up and hurried to the door just as Lord and Lady Richardson and the wife of the younger Richardson, Suzanne, whose husband was tied up in Parliament, and their nephew Kenneth Thompson who stated his parents were slightly delayed by his younger brother having broken his arm the day before.

All right, Kenneth was here…didn't matter about anything else. Isn't she awful. She did keep her wits about her enough to commiserate on Andrew's accident and asked if it was a serious break or not….evidently not, more a crack but he was most uncomfortable and they were waiting for some pain medication to take effect before setting out for the Glass Castle.

A great commotion occurred next with the arrival of Lord and Lady Baden, including their son, the twin new babies, a nurse and a maid – Elizabeth knew Henry was no problem. Right behind them was a carriage with Lady Dierdre Morton and her daughter, her new baby, her mother, Lady Madge Thompson, a nurse and a maid, with apologies from Lord Reginald Thompson – being on Parliamentary business. Lady Dierdre apologized also but her husband, Lord Edward Morton, was also tied up in Parliament – Elizabeth assuming they must be working with the young Sir Richardson on something.

The next three carriages were some of the young men and young women she had met at school with their parent or parents and one brought a young sibling who immediately took the oldest Baden child's cookie and created a commotion to be heard throughout the neighborhood! Of course, Lady Jane Baden had everything under control by quickly presenting another cookie to Henry and then cautioning the grabbing child to ask her for one the next time he was so hungry. The parent of the thief was most chagrined and apologized profusely and Lady Jane, in her calm and pleasant manner said group affairs were hard on young children and it didn't matter in the least. Everyone around smiled but Elizabeth realized Lady Jane was not feeling as calm as she sounded, Elizabeth knowing none of Jane's children would EVER grab a cookie from anyone, being the most well-brought-up children, she had ever seen.

Four more carriages arrived, all filled to the brim with people including among them Lord and Lady Moore and Tyson, her piano "student". Several arrived by horseback including Doctor Josiah Ormond and Elizabeth's attorney, Lord Edward Ambrose.
Elizabeth was getting tired with all the greeting and hand shaking but realized her parents were also very busy getting everyone into the house and keeping watch on the one boy who continued to misbehave – evidently stealing cookies was not his only vice,

since he had tried to put his hand in the fruit compote and had successfully stolen a finger-full of cake icing. Had they never corrected this disreputable child at all!?! She so wanted them to take him home but guessed she couldn't say so.

She was at her wits-end, she could not enjoy the company for worrying about that awful youngster. Just as she was about to toss him out, Kenneth went up to him, picked him up in the air and took him outside. She followed and watched. Kenneth put him down but would not let him run back to his mother. He proceeded to talk to him for some time.

"Finally, the boy began to cry and she heard Kenneth say: "That isn't going to do any good. You can cry all night for what I care. You are to behave when you are at someone else's house. Now if you feel you can be a gentleman, I will let you go back to the party but if you cannot promise me to do so, I will have to ask your mother to take you home."

The boy sat down on the ground and said: "I didn't want to come. I wanted to stay home and play with my new dog. Can I have a piece of that cake if I stay?"

"Only if you behave yourself and not put your fingers in the cake and not take anyone else's treats."

"I promise, don't tell father when you see him, please don't tell father! He may take my new dog away."

"I won't tell your father unless you are bad again. Then I will personally take you home AND tell your father why."

The child backed up from Kenneth all the way to the porch and then ran into the house and sat on the first tread of the upstairs flight, watching Kenneth very carefully!

"Oh, how wonderful you are - you handled that so skillfully. Thank you Kenneth!"

"It paid to have had a younger brother, although in fairness to Tom he was nothing like that little monster. Come, I don't think anyone can eat that cake until you cut it, so I'll escort you and therefore get the first piece." he said laughing. Of course, he actually handed out pieces of cake for her, first to the ladies and then the attentive children.

The invitations had said for anyone to come and have nuncheon and school celebration cake but please give to their favorite charity instead of bringing Elizabeth any gifts…a request she had made and was adamant about.

After everyone took some food from the buffet and she had cut the elaborate cake, with one fingerprint in the icing, she announced that there would be tours of the new school she was opening for farm children and indigent town children. She made mention of her sincere thanks for the many contributions of school supplies she had received and gave a special

207

thanks to Kenneth Thompson for his hours and hours of help to get the school ready.

There had been many oohs and aahs when touring the school and it seemed everyone attending did so, much to the surprise of Elizabeth! After she explained all the help she had received from staff, especially their Jim, Kenneth Thompson and others – many congratulated those people on their good works and help.

CHAPTER SIXTEEN

A number of the attendees stated they would send children of their employees and see if certain neighborhood children would be interested and could ride together with others. What a great idea. By the time anyone interested had signed the book she had laid out to list interested students, it looked like the school would be full with the ones Elizabeth also knew would come from Glass Castle staff homes, or a few neighborhood children she had contacted or whose relatives had told her about.

Dr. Ormond came up to her and hugged her tightly and said it was by far the best thing he had ever heard of and he would be pleased to be most helpful in any way. He could, for free of course, give instructions on sanitation and first aid – greatly lacking among many uneducated people. He would also provide a first aid kit for the school to use, children being what they are and nicks and cuts happening easily. She hadn't thought of that need and thanked him profusely.

The mother of the incorrigible boy, offered to provide some reading books – like beginning readers, which her son had now finished, and also any supplies Elizabeth lacked, just let her know. Elizabeth asked didn't she want to keep the books for any other child she might have – because once used by the school they would get worn in a hurry. The woman looked down at her son and then said "No, I don't believe we will be having another child." Elizabeth was proud of herself when she didn't laugh.

Lady Jane Baden congratulated her heartily and although she and Sir Jonathan had already contributed the money for some of the slates, she said she had Jim unload two boxes of children's books and reference books from her carriage when they arrived. Some were from her and some from her father Lord Morton and his new bride, the former Lady Furness, and she didn't know where they had been put but they were somewhere about. While talking she had one child on a hip and Jonathan the other twin in a similar position. Elizabeth grinned at them and tickled their tummies and although quite shy, they laughed. About then their little Henry came up and thanked Elizabeth without prompting and she told him she was so very pleased he had come. To which comment he laughed and said the cake was REALLY good!

Elizabeth called Jim over and asked that he go to the kitchen and have some of the cake wrapped up and put in the carriage of the Baden's for their children to enjoy.

Finally, as light was waning, everyone climbed into carriages and with much waving and calling

210

"Goodbye!" pulled away from the house. As Elizabeth turned to see where Kenneth had gone, he came up behind her and almost scared her to death. He grinned the handsome grin and said he was going to have to leave but would be back for the first day of classes to help in any way…such as tying children to benches or generally causing confusion! She laughed and said she looked forward to seeing him but he could be put in the corner as well as any other bad boy.

"I left a present for your achievement with your Father and he said he would give it to you when things calmed down – if they did!" and laughing he kissed her forehead as he had done before and mounted his horse, which had been tied to the back of his family's carriage when they arrived.

She watched his tall, handsome person ride off, such good posture, head held high. Oh, my, she was in serious trouble. She may be young but what she felt was for a lifetime….she could only dream he felt the same. She was certain she loved him!

Within about half an hour or so everyone had left and she could breathe. She went in search of her father, so afraid the day had been too much for him. It had included over twice the number of people she had thought. On her way to find him, she stopped by the kitchen and told them how wonderful they were, the food delicious and so much extra work. She really appreciated it! They grinned and told her it was fun. Not as much work as they would have thought and that Lady Jane Baden and Lady Dierdre Morton had helped them a lot, stirring things, dishing things, and carrying back and forth. Well, how about that. Two ladies of the realm and working in the kitchen. That certainly deserved something extra…She would send boxes of chocolates – everyone loved those and they were so hard to get…with such a huge tariff on chocolate now many stores didn't carry them because few except the rich could afford any.

She found her father in the library in his favorite chair with his eyes shut and Ruth reading to him. They heard her come in and he smiled and said he was just resting a little but felt well and had enjoyed the day so very much. He had talked with Lord Richardson extensively and they were discussing the situation in the army hospitals and the Lord said he would immediately see to increasing the funding there to provide better meals, care and cleaner bedding. Her father said his bed was not changed weeks at a time, while he was there and the sheets were stiff with body fluids and dirt. She realized he meant urine as well as perspiration and it made her nauseous just thinking about it. Anyone with open wounds could die of the infections being in contact with such dirt.

"Oh, Father I am so glad you had that conversation. Couldn't I do something? How about I send some new sheets, blankets and mattresses to the one where you were for so long?"

"Oh, Daughter that would be marvelous. Do you not mind, when your school will take so much money from your accounts?"

"No indeed, I will go and write to him this very evening so it can be mailed in the morning. I pretty well know the costs because I have just furnished the dormitory for the school. How many beds were there – do you have any idea?"

"Oh, well, I would think – let's see – 12 rooms and 20 in a room – 240?"

"Oh, my goodness, so much pain and trouble! Well, that is certainly more than I would have guessed but not a number I cannot accommodate. If I send twice that, they can change the bedding. I will go and write the letter now. I am so very fortunate and my solicitors have increased my holdings a couple times over in the nine years – it will be well. I can provide that number and will notify some others of the need too, for there are eight army hospitals I believe. That way they can have the pleasure of helping with replacements too."

He found he was tearful when she left the room. How could he be so very blessed with such a daughter? He hoped she wasn't mistaken in the fact others will help also. He didn't know that he had that much faith in people…but maybe he was too disgruntled…out of the mouths of babes: 'They could have the pleasure?' Had she really said that? He certainly hoped it wasn't naïve, but he was afraid it was indeed a pipe dream.

Oh, he had so underestimated his daughter! At that very minute she was writing to: The Badens, The Mortons, Dr. Ormond, The Richardsons – two generations, The Prescotts, The Huffmans, of course the Thompsons and laid her pad aside to think of others, and she eventually added six more letters.
Her letters were short and to the point. She had found out that the weeks her father had been in the military hospital his bed had not been frequently changed. She was not aware of all conditions but would take care of the Reed hospital herself – where the Major had been but there were seven other military hospitals, that she knew of. She was appealing to some of her many friends for them to help with mattresses and bedding.
Elizabeth had written all the letters that night staying up quite late although tired from her party. With mailings the next morning, she felt it would be a couple weeks before she would hear anything, if at all….huh…little did she know!

On the eighth day after her mailing a huge carriage drew up to the door of the Glass House. The butler was alarmed because the seal of the king was on the door of the carriage.   He immediately sent Julie to fetch the Major and Mistress to come and greet whoever was arriving.

Elizabeth stood behind the Butler as he invited the man, who wore a lot of gold braid and fancy clothes, to enter.   She bowed and introduced herself as Elizabeth Masters, how could she be of help?

"Well, Humm, you are exactly the person I seek. May I present to you a letter from King George and a letter from Parliament, My Dear?" (Fleetingly she wondered why they didn't use the post as everyone else did.)

Curtseying, she said "Certainly, Sir."

"His majesty is aware of your concern for our honorable service members and particularly those injured in the line of duty. He is most interested in the conditions of the military hospitals and would like you informed that a Parliamentary Committee, headed by Lord Richardson has been authorized to look into the situation immediately.   They are to report back to the King within a fortnight with their recommendations on the conditions of such hospitals and request the King's authorization of the amount of money needed to correct the situation.

With His Grace's best wishes, I thank you.   In this envelope you will find a letter directly to you from the King with this information. Good day to you, My Dear!" And he left…before she could get her parents here or anything. They would think she had lost her mind, if she didn't have the butler and the letter, complete with gold seal, to prove it!

Behind her she could hear Walter, the new butler, saying "Oh, Dear! Oh, Dear! I have never!"

Laughing and breathless, she said "Well, Walter, I have never either!"

About that time her Father came into the hall and said he thought he had seen the King's carriage leaving the driveway. Had they had some kind of trouble and needed assistance, or why were they here?

Elizabeth just handed him her letter and Walter immediately starting talking very loud and very fast about what had just occurred.

Alfred hollered for Ruth – totally unlike him. Then he took the nearest chair – a quite uncomfortable model beside the front door – not really expected to have anyone sit on it.

"Elizabeth, child, what have you done? Is the King displeased? What have you stirred up? I thought you were just asking some friends for sheets. What have you done?"

She sat on the stairs and started to cry. That is where Ruth came into it – looking from one to the other and then the fancy, closed letter in a huge envelope complete with the crown's seal.

"Oh, Dear Girl. Whatever is the matter? Did you write to the King?"

"I did not! I only wrote to friends asking them to take on the other seven hospitals for sheets, mattresses or blankets – my having ordered for the eighth hospital that Father used. I had no intention of making the whole of England aware. And the king's coach at our door. And his own messenger talking to me! And a letter on the King's stationary sent to me? Oh, Lord, what have I done!?!"

"Hush, Darling, it cannot be anything bad. No gendarmes came…only the King's messenger. It must be a thank you note or something. Lord Richardson is quite close to the King and even eats an occasional meal at the palace. It cannot be anything bad at all, he would not have sent his own messenger with a reprimand. He would have sent a military person."

Before anyone could open the epistle, there was a knock on the front door. A very exhausted looking Kenneth stood there. "Oh, I see from your faces I am too late. I was just told hours ago, by Grandfather, that the King was going to send you a letter of congratulations for your interest in helping his troops and I wanted to ease the surprise a little….it looks like I may be late?"

Elizabeth rushed to him, crying onto his coat lapel. "Oh, thank you for coming, I am beside myself and haven't had the courage to open the letter yet. Will you please stay and read it with me?"

"Of course, Angel, I will stay!"

Ruth rang for refreshments to be brought to the Library and they headed that way as well, Alfred

217

taking his reading chair, Ruth the one close beside him where she often read as well and Elizabeth and Kenneth on the settee. Slowly and carefully, she opened the official seal on the envelope and took out the gold embossed note paper with handwritten ink message.

"Mistress Masters, your humble servant, I, Kind George, wish to thank you for your generous help in outfitting the army hospital at Andrews. It has come to my attention, because of your good works, that we have been extremely remiss in our care of the veterans of our campaign against France, and possibly from other wars as well. Please know that as of this date I have ordered sufficient funds be spent by Parliament on the condition of each of the eight army hospitals and any other such facilities that may require better treatment! Your generosity and caring have brought your King to his knees with gratitude and shame. Your humble servant, The Righteous and Honourable King George III."

They all sat transfixed! Finally, Kenneth got his voice back first and said well, he was certainly keeping company with an important person now. An actual letter from the reclusive King…that should be framed. Alfred laughed and said only his daughter would get the attention of King George. And Ruth said – "You see, Darling, how your good works are recognized and you deserve it. This is so very nice!"

Kenneth cleared his throat and said: "I don't know if I qualify anymore to keep company with such an important person, but if she will grant me the privilege to accompany her, I could be persuaded to go for a short ride before nuncheon. Am I invited to stay for nuncheon, Major Masters?"

"You must know you are always welcome in this house Kenneth. And any meal we have we will gladly share with you…Why don't you two go ride a short while and we'll see about the nuncheon menu while you're gone."

Putting on her riding boots from the back hall closet, Elizabeth said she was ready to ride in her day dress. She grabbed a sweater from the closet also and she headed for the barn while Kenneth went out the front and brought his horse around.

It was a lovely day with just a hint of the fall air to come. Her horse had not been ridden as much lately, what with the school and the party so he was very spirited but she was an excellent rider and gave the horse his head enough to tire him out a bit. Kenneth mostly kept up with her but had to grin at her enthusiasm to ride fast and furious. So, like her, dive in and get it done! He couldn't believe the school opened next week…how she had done it he couldn't know…although he had been in on a lot of the construction, she had lessons, teachers, and a lot of students all organized and scheduled already.

He was to tell her today that his mother would bring cookies and hand cakes the first school day as a surprise. He loved her hand cakes with a filling of fruit or nuts. He hoped she would keep a few at home for him. Childish as it was he still craved his Mother's cooking. They had always had servants to do most of it but she so enjoyed being in the kitchen that she often did a good bit of the preparation herself. Elizabeth reminded him of his mother …her industry and the urge to forge ahead and get things done.

CHAPTER SEVENTEEN

The school was indeed the busiest place Elizabeth had ever been…much more abuzz than any she had ever attended. Many of the students had no idea what to do, never being in a school before and she was tickled to see, although wearing normal and patched clothes, their hair was slicked down with water and their faces and hands clean as could be.

One little fellow came up and said: "Missus, I's not been to school before and I's can't read. Do I have to go back home or can I stay for those cookies over there?"
Oh, Goodness! Well, bless his baby heart. "What is your name, Sweetheart?" "It is Tommy, Miss, Tommy Woodward." "Oh Tommy, you are supposed to be here, Dear. We will teach you to read and do maths. And the cookies are for everyone who stays plus there will be a nuncheon too!"

"Oh, Missus, you mean food in the middle of the day? I had me porridge this morning but didn't expect no food until dark. We's don't eat no nuncheon at our house."
Trying very hard not to cry, she said: "Well, Dear, you will have nuncheon here at the school every day

you attend. It may only be meat and bread and a piece of fruit but it will be nuncheon, none the less."

"Oh, Missus, I's so glad to come. Will I learn to read? Ma said I may learn to read and can teach her! She started in the mine and then went to the factory and now washes and cleans. She's been workin' since she was five Ma'am."
"Well, Dear, you will learn to read and do sums and some other things too. And have lunch and have papers to take home to read to your Ma – when you learn enough. Now come and have a seat so we can get started today. There are classrooms upstairs but we will start here today. You find a seat anywhere you like."

She managed to swallow her tears and saw Ruth, Lady Caroline Thompson with two huge baskets of treats, the minister's wife, her Father, and about six others all helping get children into seats and answering questions or nodding at excited explanations like she had gotten from little Tommy. She saw Ruth swallowing hard – well, she wasn't the only one almost in tears.

It took a little while to get the children settled but none were acting out she was glad to see and all seemed shy but excited.

She went to the front and only then wondered where "her" Tom had gotten to. He had arrived at dawn and with Big Jim had a fire started to take off the chill and had been standing by to assist many of the scared but excited children to take seats on the benches. Finally, she saw him come in carrying a little blonde girl in ragged dress who had obviously been crying. He was whispering to her and she was holding very tightly to his ear! Ellie had to smile…what she wouldn't give for a picture of that – if only she could paint, but her art skills were very poor.

She looked to the front corner where his mother was helping with foods and saw the good woman watching her son and also teary eyed. She winked when Lady Thompson looked up. They smiled at each other and watched Tom help the little girl sit on a bench next to another girl who made room for her, so was obviously going to be pleasant.

Drawing in a shaky breath, she went to the front and smiling said she was so very glad they had come to this school. They were going to read, write and do maths and would have nuncheon and snacks. If any of them needed to go to the out-house, it was in the back behind the building and they had permission to get up and go out, there would be a big man named Jim who could help them. They were to come right back in, wash their hands in the basin at the back door and take their seats again. Many looked alarmed when she mentioned washing their hands, probably a very unusual practice for many.

She asked if any had done letters or numbers or even reading before and five of the twenty said they had. She said that was good and they could be helpful to others who had not but would have their school upstairs once the new students were settled in a day or two. She uncovered a large slate easel that Tom had built for her and on it she had twelve letters and ten numbers.

Starting with these letters, she would sound them out and explain a common word that used such letter to start it. After going through this several times, she then asked the students to say it when she pointed but didn't say it for them. That got a great response. She then did the same with the numbers.

She thanked a few students who had been assisting others. She then called upon various students to say a word that started with that letter sound but not the same word already used. This took some doing but before long even the most uneducated of the group could understand and come up with a word like horse and house or cat and cup or dog and dish. She said the next day the students who knew the charts would go upstairs to a regular classroom and have a teacher there to help them.

Those just learning would stay down here a while longer until they knew the whole alphabet, basic numbers and could put small words together.

A couple times she was interrupted by more children coming in and last count Tom made there were 31 students! More than some small schools. By mid-morning there was a little squirming going on and she said they would take a break. Each child could take a turn going to the outhouse and after hand washing, they would get a snack. Well, that certainly got a lot of attention!

She was impressed that most were very polite and none were pushing another. The ladies had put out trays of cookies, sliced apples and hand cakes. There were metal cups of milk, cider, and water. About equally enjoyed by the children. One little boy said he loved milk and got it when he went to Gramps. Wherever that was, it was obviously from his voice - a great place to go. The snack was thoroughly enjoyed and everyone was encouraged to take a seat again and they would get nuncheon later. Some, like the boy that morning, could not believe they would get something more to eat.

The balance of the morning was given up to alphabet and numbers with examples, children called on, those who volunteered, or simply those so excited that they announced the answer unasked. Elizabeth was exhausted but enjoying herself immensely.

Some examples by holding up one apple, then another, followed by a third and the children calling out one, two or three. Some were learned beyond such basics but a good many had no information at all. By lunch time the class had increased to 35.

As the students were told nuncheon would be served soon, they were all chattering, bragging about what they knew, or asking questions. Quite an active group from the solemn and quiet children of that morning. Elizabeth announced they could go to the yard and pet two horses, two cats, and have a quick look around but not to wander off or they would miss the meal. The poor little waif from this morning stood close to Elizabeth and anywhere she moved to help get the nuncheon organized he was right there. She decided to give him jobs to do. Asking him to wash his hands, which he did without argument, she then made him help put out the metal bowls she had ordered for each child to use to accumulate whatever they picked to eat. She must remember to tease Ruth, who had said she was overly optimistic when she ordered from a bar supplier, 4 sets of 10 bowls. There were small pieces of fried chicken, small slices of ham, apple slices, two kinds of sliced bread, and slices of vegetables – some raw and some cooked.

They were told those who returned a clean plate would get a cookie or hand pie.

The afternoon went much as the morning but thankfully not as long for she was exhausted and her helpers looked the same.

Alfred had gone back to rest at nuncheon but had come in and helped in the afternoon with the lessons, moving among the children and correcting their slates and explaining what was correct or if not why. He was so patient and the children while very afraid of him at first for his missing arm and limp but by evening were clustering around him, seeking his help and grinning.

Tom also had a cluster of children and was likewise correcting work and making suggestions, praising any little accomplishment. His mother helped, Ruth helped and Mrs. Edna Prim from the village, who had been enthusiastic from the first rumor of the school also had a group seeking her help. A few of the other neighborhood ladies helped children or straightened out the food table and cleaned the bowls.

Although not a teacher herself Edna said her mother and sister had been and she told Elizabeth she was having the time of her life and couldn't wait for the next day! Although quite old, she had ridden her horse to the Glass Castle. Living not too far from the estate. Jim told her on a rainy day he would pick her up in the buggy.

227

About an hour before the finish of the day, Doris, the kitchen supervisor and her staff brought out fresh cool tea and some more cookies. These children would be bouncing off the walls this evening from all the unusual sugar but adults thought the offering was gold plated from the excitement of the children. Elizabeth told them this was today only for showing up for the first day but she hoped they had enjoyed themselves and to be careful going home.

A number of older brothers or sisters or parents had shown up to escort their little ones. Tom had gone out and hitched the surrey and was waiting for those who didn't have a way because of parents still working or simply disinterested. The poor little boy who had shadowed Elizabeth all day was picked up by a woman in worse shape than he and she quickly asked if the woman would help her by taking some of the left-over food. She explained she had overestimated the students' hunger and hated for it to go to waste. She wasn't certain the woman believed her but with great thanks took the wrapped bundle and walked hand in hand down the lane. Mrs. Prim came up and said they lived behind her and the woman took in washing and it was just the two of them as far as any neighbor knew.

Like a carrot to a horse, thought Alfred, who overheard, he could see the wheels turning in Elizabeth's head and knew for certain his daughter would find the woman a job at the estate. She would have found it commendable for the woman to be interested in her son getting an education, no matter how hard her life or having to walk him to and from each day. Mrs. Prim rushed up to the woman as the two were leaving and said why didn't he come to her house and ride on the horse with her each morning and evening. His mother was adamant with her thanks and the boy was excited to actually ride a horse.

As the school emptied, Elizabeth sat on the first bench and cried. She cried for ten minutes, twelve minutes, quarter of an hour. Tom, Alfred and Ruth were so very concerned.

Tom sat down beside her putting his arm about her shoulders. "You did it, Sweetheart, you did it. How great was this day! And 35 students…even if a few do not return – what an achievement. I would have thought ten would have been a satisfactory number….think of all these poor children who would not have been to school today without YOU. I am so very proud!"

Although it was quite improper she buried her head in his shoulder and cried for another five minutes or thereabout.

"I, I, I feel so fortunate. I feel so overwhelmed. What if I can't impart enough knowledge for them…what if it is all a failure and I let these poor little beings down? Oh, Tom, what have I done?"

"You have provided a window into a whole world of possibilities for them. If half don't return, it is the half you help that matter. They would have had no chance without YOU! Do not worry about the number that come or don't. Just keep on with your plan. You have so many people who wish to help teach and to show things of interest to them. You have all those books to use…you will see…it will be well."

Her father came up and said: "Enough of this crying Elizabeth. There are things to be done and people to thank. Come away from Tom a minute and take care of things so these tired people who have helped you so generously can go home. It has been a very long day for all of us. Let's get it to an end and plan for tomorrow. I feel you need to hire someone to help in the kitchen or maybe even two. Those ladies have worked so strenuously – baking once, then baking again. And the nuncheon they provided was fit for a king. Come, Dear, let's see about finishing up in here and heading for the house to relieve staff a bit."

Immediately, rising and apologizing to Tom and her Father, she did indeed organized the closing of the school for the day. She checked the outhouse and found it not in the terrible condition she had feared. Using the cleaning materials including lime for the hole, from a small cabinet, it didn't take but a minute to set it to rights. She then came back in and helped

230

Lady Thompson and Ruth finish clearing up the food serving area. Her father, one arm notwithstanding, had taken care that the fire was out and the fireplace brushed and logs ready at the side for the next morning. My goodness, she hoped none of the children were sick tonight, what a conglomeration of food they had consumed. She expected there to be cookies, hand cakes, and vegetables left over but hardly any remained. She had to be very stern with herself to not cry again, realizing how hungry her students had been.

As they worked to finish up and have things in order for the next day, Lady Thompson came up and said: "Elizabeth you are a wonder indeed. I am so very proud of you…can you believe over thirty students came? I cannot countenance it. Now tomorrow we will have more help for I will bring my Grace and Edith with me and they can manage a crowd with one hand tied behind them….it will be easier on Ruth and Alfred, and of course you, to have more help. They are both educated enough to assist with books and things too. I believe I can do without them at home for many days, except at holiday or if I plan a large party – do not worry about that."
"Well, thank you so much. I am going to hire the mother of that little Tom who clung to me all day. She can help in the kitchen at the house since I have put such a burden on them to fix so much food. I

231

had not expected so many children in my wildest dreams. Even if several do not come tomorrow, think what a great door is being opened to the ones who do…I am so pleased!"

"As well you should be. I am aware that my son Tom loves you very much and this just reinforces the pleasure his father and I have in his choice. You are everything we could have wished for him, Elizabeth."

On that comment, she could not say a word…she was speechless as unusual as that may be.

Ruth then came up and asked if she, Elizabeth, had eaten today? She gave her an odd look and then said, "No, except for a hand pie and some carrots, I don't believe I have." then she laughed.

Turning too quickly she staggered and Big Jim was standing there and caught her before she could fall. "Miss Elizabeth, you must eat when the children do, and let some of the others of us check the out-house and bring in firewood. You need to sit down once in a while and eat something too. You are the backbone of this school and must not get sick or overly tired. You do not want to be the one that hinders the teachings."

Well, nothing like being dressed down by your barn manager. But she had to laugh, he had been looking out for her since she was two years old. It was nice that he cared. Realizing all this, she thanked him with her dimpled grin and he felt well-paid.

There were very tired people that evening. Little supper was eaten by Elizabeth, Alfred or Ruth. Bedtime came before dark and all three were asleep when their heads hit the pillows. They had said elaborate goodbyes to the several helpers and watched as Kenneth out-road his mother's carriage – although they knew he was very tired, how gracious of him to escort his mother.

Elizabeth rose in the night worried she had forgotten something or some child had been left with no way home. After realizing she had checked that and there was no need to worry, she finally fell back to sleep.

The next day dawned and she was in the school after her tea and crumpet. It was just barely sunup and students started coming in. Not the least of which was Little Tom. She quickly got to his mother, who had walked him today not waiting for Edna Prim to take him, and she asked Mrs. Woodward. if she was interested in a job in the Glass Castle kitchens. Well, yes she would love a job, what did it pay? Elizabeth said 3 shillings per day and food for both her and Tom. She was aghast and had to sit down. "Oh, Miss Elizabeth, oh I would be so honored. I do not have nice clothes to work in such a house, however. I am afraid I must decline until I can get a better garment." She said, almost in tears.

"Oh, no need, we have uniforms we furnish. Quite nice ones with aprons and all. I am certain we can fit you with one and next we order you will have two with your name as other staff do…one for wearing while one is washed. Oh, and what is your name, I can't just call you Tom's mother", she said laughing. "Alice, mam. Alice Woodward."

Well, tarnation she had made the poor soul cry. Patting her back, she said not to worry, she would have Jim escort her to the house and have Lucy show her what to do and loan her a uniform for the day – if she could start today?" Nodding yes while sobbing, Elizabeth told her to stay there until Jim came to take her to the kitchens. Elizabeth left to go back inside to talk with Jim and have him explain what was happening to the kitchen staff.

It was almost time to start the lessons but she took a second to tell little Tom that his mother was now working in their kitchens for pay and he would be allowed to stay at the house after school, until it was time for his mother to go home…just prior to supper.

Days sped by and all went as planned. The normal number of students being 30. The formal teachers for the upstairs were scheduled well and had classes in mathematics, spelling, vocabulary, literature, history, and a number of smaller sessions on health, mapping, naval operations, careers, Parliament, laws, and especially farming – to include fertilizer, drainage, planting, fruit, harvesting, and proper storage of grains and grasses to avoid mold or other damage to the crops. There were four wanting farming classes – she had thought she might have one.

Some of the really interesting days included the sheriff speaking on being a deputy, Lord Richardson on laws, wars and Parliament (which had the boys eyes agog!), and Dr. Ormond on it being important to keep things clean, on attending wounds and scrapes, and recognizing serious illness by checking fever and thirst.

The beginning learners on the first floor made great headway toward understanding mathematics, making change, counting, denominations of money; washing things and themselves well; and spelling and reading; it was interesting that many wanted to do well to get to move to the "upstairs" classes – an advantage that Elizabeth had not considered but was reasonable in fact.

After over two months of classes, Elizabeth had the "upper" students write what they had found most interesting (1), most helpful to their future (2), and most generally useful (3).

School was such a tremendous success that Elizabeth was constantly reminding herself of how fortunate she was to have so much help. Tom's mother had been as devoted as even Ruth and she was amazed at how the lady thought of things to do in assisting her. The staff Lady Armstrong provided were also very helpful…willing to do whatever was needed.

Of the more advanced students, it was obvious that although most had done well in regular classes including good test scores, the various speakers added the most information that the students found interesting. For the next school year, she would try her best to have as many special speakers as she could. She even asked her father if he would discuss war and surviving - including injuries. Elizabeth would have her banker come to talk about money and savings. And she had scheduled Dr. Ormond for more time the next session too.

As the first and second anniversary of the 5-month sessions and opening of the Glass Castle school passed it was found to have turned out a goodly number of youth educated enough to get jobs that paid sufficiently to be more than a bare existence and the families were benefitting in better gardens, better income, better food and just BETTER! She would never have dreamed that so little class time could provide so much learning but the students were so very underlined.

Another kitchen helper and another cook had been added to the staff at the Castle and the meals continued to be of great interest to the students…many of the beginners eating their best meal of the day during classes. Mrs. Woodward was an excellent help in the kitchen and learned easily like her son. Staff were quite pleased with her. She was untutored in cooking but they said they could teach her with little problem – she is a quick learner, just inexperienced.

Another lady from the church expressed interest when the Minister's wife had said a position was available so the kitchen would now be staffed sufficiently for the added burden of the student lunches and treats.

CHAPTER EIGHTEEN

The school year with its two sessions had progressed well and was far more successful than Elizabeth had even hoped.

That spring, Lady Jane Baden had her brother Lord Edward Morton invite Elizabeth – accompanied by her companiable Sir Kenneth Thompson with her father and Ruth as chaperones – to come to Parliament and discuss her school and the impact it had on the neighborhood and the country in general. That education of the masses was not a detriment to society and could provide great help to the populace. New ideas for certain! From the looks on some of the faces of the older members, it was a wasted breath but she had great support from some of the younger ones and was satisfied, knowing it was always hard to change people's minds and habits.

On a personal level, Elizabeth was having a big party, not of her doing but she didn't refuse her parents' wishes. To celebrate the success of her school, her parents had planned it while she had been so very busy with the class preparation, her speech to Parliament, learning about her wealth and investments, courtesy of Sir Edward Ambrose, Esq., and estate issues that she had just been glad to survive all the activity.

As usual, she was opposed to a big celebration but they were determined and she didn't have the heart to spoil what was turning into a joyous planning event for the two parents.

Her school now had a steady 28 students on average with 20 being in the advanced section and 8 to 10 or so regularly in the primary section. It was a manageable number and over the year some of the beginners were now already in the advanced section and four of the advanced had moved on to public institutions of learning after their first year here. Hopefully to eventually go to trade schools or universities – much sooner than she would have ever imagined.

That had been helped with the special tutors who provided specific attention in certain areas the young people were weakest. And scholarship money for continuing education given by many of the affluent friends of Elizabeth. Things to prepare for college were offered many times with Doctor Ormond providing medical texts, and many other "swells", including Sir Edward Morton and Sir Thomas Richardson, providing texts or journals on law, economics, finance, and other complicated subjects – which gave the students enough start to pass entrance examinations in higher echelons of education.

All told a phenominal year indeed!

Locally some improvement had been seen on farms and small businesses where they could get knowledgeable help with certain issues that related to their being more successful. Mathematics had been the most popular, with every business needing such expertise and educated staff in any kind of calculation, from money to sizing to counting to more complicated issues – like construction, sales, and quantities. The classes in farming were so very successful that additional had been added. Not too much of the experimental things like the Summerwood Estate or some others tried. But the hard and true farming or orchard operations with known fertilizers, and how to properly apply them were popular.

Too often someone heard of a product, bought it, and spread it out not knowing that it had to be mixed with the soil, diluted with water or added at a certain stage of production. Lord Morton, Lady Jane Baden's father had loaned his estate manager to teach a two-day class once a month. He would travel in an evening, spend two nights at the Glass Castle and provide farm management classes. He also loaned his orchardist on occasion. This got attendance from some students who were older but working on farms and whose employers saw the advantage of a better educated farm hand. It was well-known that the Morton estate had superior crops and production totals and owners were anxious to replicate that success. Not common, of course, but if she could help a half dozen it was certainly a good thing, wasn't it? And it soon became apparent that such classes would have six or seven farm men attend every time.

Unlike a "regular" school, certain classes could be taken and not a whole day or whole curriculum. Just what that student needed. Little Tommy Woodward was a good example of the school teaching an interested pupil. His mother had flourished by having a regular job and pay in the kitchens at the Glass Castle and the child, himself, had learned much quicker than most others, progressing to a third-grade reader in one year and was a whiz at his numbers. Now he was bigger and "braver" he would work at odd jobs for Doctor Ormond two afternoons a week in exchange for instruction in medications, wounds and such. He hoped when he reached his teens to get a job in a convalescent home or an army hospital. He loved helping people and Doctor Ormond was very impressed in all he was learning.

Now her school had made it for two school sessions, it was hard to tell who was the most excited, Alfred,

Ruth, Elizabeth, or Kenneth. Kenneth had already spoken to her father and had permission to ask the BIG question, diamond ring burning a hole in his pocket for the last two weeks! He would have liked to ask her a year ago but with the school keeping her so exhausted and busy, his parents had encouraged him to put it off. Kenneth didn't think she had a clue but it was always hard to tell what Elizabeth was thinking. So much on her mind...so many helpful things for others!

There was to be a party to celebrate the school finishing a double semester of classes. Students that had completed any full course at the Glass Castle had been invited. Current students had been invited. Both sets of invitations stating NO presents but bring food or clothing to be distributed to the needy if they could – which would meet with Elizabeth's approval her parents were certain. Anyone who couldn't bring something was encouraged to attend anyway...the object being to show Elizabeth how much she and her school were loved and appreciated.

The staff at the estate were beyond happy...a lot of extra work but they were enthused at the prospect of doing something for "their girl" when she had done so much for others...including making certain staff had learned to read and do their numbers...holding small classes in the evening or mornings – whatever

242

worked in their schedules – she hadn't forgotten them – they wouldn't forget her.

It was just getting sunup and the birthday girl was at present up to her elbows in planting soil and flowers, deciding just two days before that the urns on the big porch and at the conservatory doors needed replanting. Henry, although getting up in years now, was enthusiastically directing the operation and three other staff were hauling bags of soil, fertilizer, watering cans and innumerable flowering plants.

Ruth came out on the porch and tut-tutted at Elizabeth. "Child, if you do not hurry and get yourself dressed better your birthday guests are going to find you in a soiled dress and apron!"

Well, tarnation! Where had the morning gone? She apologized to the workers, although they were almost finished, and she hurried up to her room where her clothes were at least laid out and a washing basin ready with warm water and soap handy. Looking in the glass she realized she was a fright of major catastrophe! Laughing, in her usual good humor, and with Julie's help, she managed to get quite presentable in a hurry. Ruth had insisted on buying her the most beautiful blue frock and with a quick wash she slipped into it. Her hair was another matter, being damp and stringy but finally piled on her head with her fanciest combs, she decided it was good enough and rushed from the room with hurried thanks to the woman who had been helping her these many years!

As people started to arrive, Elizabeth became alarmed and asked Kenneth how many had been invited. He said he understood 100 but that would include one invitation per household. Holy Cow! One hundred invitations? Yes, he said, he believed that was the number. He and his mother had helped Ruth address many of them while Alfred stuffed envelopes or folded and fastened each item with wax since his penmanship was almost unreadable with only his left hand.

Well, Thank Heaven the weather was very nice and the yard prepared so that the house didn't have to hold them all, she thought. She had wondered why the ball room, which hadn't been used much in several years had been cleaned and drapery changed but hadn't asked…now she knew why. Peaking in she noticed tables with food along one whole wall and any number of chairs and stools arranged around the room. Her piano teacher from years past was playing the piano in the music room with the doors open between and she hurried forward and hugged her. Liking the baby grand piano sound as she always did and glad she wasn't the one playing it – for she was not really good yet, serviceable but not professional, with so much else on her mind than piano practice..

244

She recognized women from the church who were arranging dozens of dishes of food on the long tables and grinning like conspirators. She thanked them all and even snatched a chicken tea sandwich, realizing she hadn't eaten except a ham biscuit with her tea at sunup. Kenneth Thompson found her and said it was time to start the party officially and if she would not mind Ruth and her father would like her to come to the foyer for a minute.

She realized she was shaking and he took her hand, patting it and telling her it was just one day and all would be well. She certainly hoped so! But tarnation she had never seen such a gathering. Even speaking to a committee in Parliament, as nervous as she had been the audience was much smaller than all this fal-de-ral! Her father and Ruth were standing on the curved staircase and when she and Kenneth entered everyone crowded in the foyer and hall (plus spilling into all adjoining rooms) and clapped. He squeezed her hand and she managed to climb up several stairsteps to be beside her father with Ruth just above. Then she turned to say a greeting.

"I am so overcome with so much good will! I appreciate you all, each and every one, for coming to help me celebrate! I know a lot of you have assisted with, heard about, or visited my school, and I want to thank you so much! Many of you in this room have provided such great help with supplies,

245

furniture, teaching sessions and last but certainly not least the piles of food we have needed – for a full belly helps an alert mind!

I cannot begin to name you all – had I known this was to be such a huge affair I would have compiled some notes...but please, all of you, realize how grateful I am at your support for the school.   I am most appreciative of you!"

Just then, as Ruth and her Father thanked everyone for coming and hoped they would find the food and music enjoyable, all of a sudden a loud blasphemy was heard from the direction of the doorway and a man with a gun fired at her father!   Everyone it seemed screamed and Kenneth along with James Richardson jumped the man as he tried to fire again but thankfully the projectile went into the hall floor. In the melee Elizabeth couldn't see if anyone was hit and then realized Ruth had blood on her shoulder and her father was slumped on the stairs!

The man that had been tackled, was shouting he had missed her, he had missed her, evidently meaning Elizabeth!

There was a lot of milling about but most seemed to realize the two men had the idiot in strong control and there was no other apparent danger.   Doctor Ormond swung his large body part-way up the stairs and announced for everyone to please go to the large ballroom where the food was until the gendarmes could come and he would attend the major. They were welcome to eat the food, but no one was to leave since they were all witnesses. Someone had already ridden to get the sheriff and any deputy on duty.

He added they were not to worry the blow was glancing and the Major would be all right but would need a bandage. Please everyone clear the foyer for now. Whereupon Doctor Ormond asked little Tommy to go to his carriage and bring his medicine bag and the red bag with the bandages.

In the haze of her distress, she noticed Jonathan Baden escorting people in the direction of the ballroom and Lady Jane Baden doing the same and tut tutting and patting and trying to calm everyone. Elizabeth in all her terror and concern for her father couldn't help but admire those two….always on top of things! She saw that Kenneth was really all right and his mother leaving him to head to the ballroom – probably to help serve food ahead of schedule. Elizabeth relaxed a little knowing Lady Thompson and her two staff could handle that situation with ease.

None of the small children here had seen the shooting, being in the study with treats and games and two nannies. Two of the gentlemen had gone that direction, probably to provide protection.

247

Kenneth had stripped off his neckerchief and used it to tie the man's hands and another man, whose name she couldn't recall in all this trauma had removed a belt and used it to restrict the man's legs. Ruth was sitting beside Alfred and patting him on the back. He managed to catch Elizabeth's eye and winked at her, smiling all the while. Oh, goodness, how brave he was! Well, it looked to be, hopefully, just a glancing blow on his bad shoulder and not in the chest or head thank the Lord Above! How dare anyone injure him, he had devoted most of his adult life to protecting the country – now to be shot by some idiot in his own home – unconscionable!

At that time, it suddenly dawned on her the man had shouted he missed "her", the only "her" there had been Ruth and Elizabeth, herself! Why in the name of sense had anyone wanted either of them shot? She had to admit that Ruth stood above them and she was beside her father....but why in tarnation would anyone want to shoot HER? She had never to her knowledge hurt anyone! Never fired any staff, testified against anyone, rarely refused to hire any – that not being her job except for the school and she had found jobs enough for anyone interested there!

How could she have possibly angered the man so severely? She didn't realize tears were rolling down her face until Ruth patted her arm and said it would be all right.

"Darling, the man is insane, and your father will be fine. It is indeed only a flesh wound – not hitting either bone nor artery nor vein."

"Oh, I am so glad, Mother, so glad. But why did he shoot? Was he aiming at ME? He shouted he "missed her", it must have been me because I was the only one beside Father! What could I have ever done to him – I've never seen him before as far as I can recollect!"

"We will know more when we find out who he is…the deputies are here and the sheriff should be along shortly, being on another call. Come and let's go into the ball room where everyone can see you are all right and we will let them know your father is not seriously hurt…is that OK?"

"Yes, but please send someone to be certain Kenneth and his friend are all right, please."

Elizabeth found no one had started to eat, so she immediately grabbed the sleeve of Kenneth's mother and whispered, "Come with me, we need to start people eating, it is hard to tell how long the sheriff will be and the food needs to be consumed! Plus, it will help to ease the tension caused by the idiot!"

Grinning at her, Lady Caroline Thompson, started shepherding people toward the table, while Elizabeth assured everyone that her father was fine and only had a scratch and the deputies had the culprit in hand. Jane and Jonathan Baden also helped guide people

249

toward the food and a great display it was indeed! This was the first Elizabeth had seen the birthday cake (for the celebration was a combination of birthday and successful school year) and what a work of art to be sure!

She stood back and watched to make certain everyone was served and the chairs were sufficient.

Suddenly she felt a hand at her waist and jumped. "Oh, Darling, I am sorry to startle you!" said Kenneth. "Come let's eat something. The doctor has finished patching up your father and he will be in as soon as he changes his jacket. The deputy has escorted the scoundrel out."

Kenneth said: "His name is Harrow and he was angry because of the farm classes and losing his man to another farm after the fellow completed the classes at the school. Quite insane and I can only imagine how quickly his employee got out of there once offered another position." And Kenneth actually laughed.

It did make her smile, as intended, and she went with him to fill a plate – although not all that hungry, she thought. She was deciding between the souffle and the chicken casserole when she jumped at a hand on her shoulder.

"Oh, Daughter, I am sorry to startle you, I should have spoken first. I am just fine, may have a bit of a pain for a few days the blighter did make a path through the top of my shoulder but Dr. Ormond assures me as long as I keep it clean it will be fine. No broken bones or such. Certainly, less hurt than I have had before!" and her Father laughed – actually laughed at the circumstance!

"Sir, I am so sorry! He went right past us and we had no inkling what was to occur! I will regret it always!" said Kenneth with chagrin.

"Young man, after all you have done for my daughter and her school, you do not have a single thing to regret. Who would have thought such would occur? He is unbalanced I am certain and such things happen…thankfully he was a very poor shot and you did capture him!" and her father had the gall to actually laugh again.

In the other room everyone was eating and talking and finally laughing and the party was in full swing. A basket at the end of the banquet table held some envelopes, Elizabeth assumed birthday cards and she had been presented a corsage by her mother.

Lady Baden (Jane) came up and said when young Henry were jumping all over the house tonight she would blame it on all the sugar because a smaller birthday cake had been prepared and placed in the children's room….her's being not at all shy about helping himself to pieces of cake and icing! Elizabeth and Tom laughed picturing the happy boy and how much upset he could probably cause when having unlimited sweet! All three had grown like weeds and seemed so happy but well-behaved with the twins still pretty much babies though. Elizabeth told Jane how lovely her family was and said it was such a pleasure to see them.

"You almost saw my Henry the other day. He heard about your school and had decided he would rather come to it than his school and was asking our Rob to hitch a team for him! Can you image? I do believe with his father's sense of direction he may have made the trip successfully but I am glad I was saved the gray hair by him not doing so! I would never, ever, have dreamt he was coming HERE!"

CHAPTER NINETEEN

As all the people had been served or served themselves from the abundance of good foods and Elizabeth had cut her beautiful birthday cake, Tom asked her if he could have a minute of her time. She was so busy concentrating on the party, she never gave it a special thought as to why and said certainly and led him out the big doors into the yard. It was getting into late afternoon and the air was clear and the sky beautiful but not nearly getting dark yet.

As they walked toward the garden bench, he asked her to sit and then knelt in front of her. She held her breath, assuming she knew what was coming and so happy she could not speak.

True to expectations he took her hand and slipped on a large diamond ring circled by blue topaz stones. "My darling Elizabeth, will you do me the very great honor of becoming my wife? I will live wherever you prefer, knowing your school is here, this would be fine if your desire. But please, please say you will marry me!"

"Oh, yes, of course! Shall we ask my Father?"

"I already have and he gave us his blessing! As did Ruth, too."

"Well, then how do your mother and father feel?"

"You can ask her, Ellie but I have never known her to work at a "school" for days and days unless she thought it was for family!" And he laughed. "My mother was very enthusiastic but said I would have to be on my toes to keep up with you! She and my father both are very pleased and will be any help to us, if needed…not that they don't think we will be just fine, but in case….! I love you very much Elizabeth!"

"Oh, Darling, I love you too! Let's go back inside and tell everyone…is that all right with you?"

"It is indeed! There will be some broken hearts, for I know several gentlemen who admire you considerably, but I am the very lucky one! You have made me very happy, Darling!"

They kissed like she had wanted to do for many months and went back in to find her parents and his.

As they approached Major Masters, he grinned broadly noticing the blush on his daughter's face. "Well, Ellie, do you have something to tell me or should I guess from your reddened face?"

"Oh, Father, I am the happiest I have ever been. Can you please bless Kenneth and I in a marriage?'

"Yes, I can indeed! Your Mother would be happy for you too, Darling. All she wanted was for you to find what we had. She often spoke of how bright you are and how accomplished for just a small girl but she hoped you would find room in your heart for love as well and I believe you have!"

As they were shaking hands, Elizabeth heard a noise and felt a great sting in her chest and immediately passed out slumping to the floor. A number of people screamed, while both Kenneth and Alfred frantically tried to see what had happened. Alfred yelled for someone to find Doctor Ormond.

Someone else called for anyone with a gun to quickly come and find the culprit. Elizabeth didn't hear any of it! Kenneth sobbed and wanted to find the perpetrator but was keeping pressure on the wound in her chest. Thankfully not in her heart but very close. What in the hell had happened? Had the deputy let the man from earlier escape?

Caroline was kneeling beside her son and taking Ellie's pulse. It was strong but weakening. Caroline looked around for help and Dr. Ormond came through the doorway, running toward them. Ruth was right behind him.

He nodded at Kenneth and told him to keep up the pressure until he told him otherwise.

Doctor Ormond then shouted: "Get me clean cloths – as clean as possible a lot of them and cut it with a clean knife into lengths of about 1 meter! Bring them immediately! Any medication to prevent infection, immediately! Someone bring a clean bedspread or coverlet- immediately and a shallow pillow or folded towel for under her head – not thick...thin but padded! IMMEDIATELY EVERYONE!!!"

He was still holding her wrist and told Kenneth her pulse was fading, he was afraid to move her, could Kenneth keep his wits about him long enough to stay and help without passing out. Kenneth nodded he could. He then suggested his mother stay to help, having helped in some surgeries and medical treatments on their estate and in the town. Doctor Ormond nodded agreement.

Dr. Ormond took surgical scissors out of his small bag and cut Elizabeth's new dress away from the wound area, instructing Kenneth to not release any pressure he was exerting on the wound, he promised not to cut him. Caroline Thompson was wiping Elizabeth's brow and putting cool damp towels across her forehead. Dr. Ormond asked that she take off Elizabeth's shoes and stockings and put warmed wraps on her legs and feet.

They were told Lord Richardson and Lord Baden had gone to try to catch the culprit who had done this dastardly deed.

Lady Jane Baden was ushering all the visitors out toward their carriages encouraging any to take food and treats as they left. The kitchen had hurriedly presented clean linen napkins to wrap any food or cake being taken. The nannie from Summerwood was taking care of small children and releasing those called for to a parent only.

256

Suddenly Elizabeth thrashed about and it was all Kenneth could do to not let up on the wound, which was still bleeding somewhat but not as hard as initially. Kenneth straddled her to help keep her still. Dr. Ormond assured him the pressure was helping and to maintain it as well as he could. He also asked Kenneth to talk to her while holding his position, calling her by name and telling her who he is and that they were taking care of her…reassurance.

Major Masters was hovering beside his prostrate daughter and talking to her in a steady voice but he himself looked about to pass out! Ruth finally got enough of the visitors cleared to come over and encourage him to take a chair she had placed close to Elizabeth so he could talk to her – whether she heard him or not was a question because except for her trying to move a few minutes prior she was way too still!.

Dr. Ormond poured whiskey he had called for into the wound to sterilize it and had done considerable stitching. He had found the bullet and removed that. Which was good to prevent further infection. Ruth reheated damp clothes and replaced the cool ones with warm. Caroline Thompson kept Elizabeth's feet warm and massaged her legs.

Kenneth was beside himself. He could tell she was still breathing but it was so extremely shallow and although the blood was not running hard from the wound he didn't know if that was because of Dr. Ormond's care, his pressure or if she was losing strength! He prayed like he had never prayed before. He had lost his great-grandmother, whom he had loved for years but she was so sick and very old, she had wished it to end and so they couldn't regret her death as much as they missed her every day.

But this was different…this was his love and a beautiful and generous lady – just starting with life, please Lord, help her! Was all this simply because of her school? Was it the same villain that had shot at her earlier…how had he gotten loose?

Time passed and Kenneth had no idea how long they had kneeled there but both his legs were now numb. A commotion was heard in the foyer and he looked up alarmed afraid the culprit had returned – if so he would cover her with his body, she was much more important and precious than he! But it was Lord Baden and Lord Richardson returning. Lord Richardson announced that the sheriff would be here shortly - they had sent a rider for him…Jonathan and he had shot the culprit….it was the same man as earlier, the sheriff would have to defend how his men had let such a danger escape!

Kenneth looked up and asked was he dead? "Yes indeed he is! If we are tried the court will have to try us both because I seriously doubt they will be able to determine which shot was fatal! We are both very good aim and had done the job right!" Said Lord Richardson.

"Congratulations, Gentlemen. Job well done! I wish I had been in on it with you, would have been better than shooting at the Frenchies, I assure you!" said Major Masters with emphasis.

"Well, we are right proud of your service, Sir and glad we could accommodate you today!"

About that time Elizabeth gave a great groan and tried to open her eyes. "Oh, Darling, lay very still, please. Dr. Ormond is here and helping you....just lay still. I am trying not to hurt you but need to keep pressure on to stop the bleeding. Please, Love, just lie still." Said Kenneth.

She looked at him with a funny expression. 'What happened? My chest hurts something awful and you are making it worse by pressing on it. Kenneth what is going on?"

"Oh, Love, you were shot in the chest. Doctor Ormond and I have been attending you for some time. Please lay still as can be. You have lost a lot of blood. You were shot in the chest by the man who shot your father earlier. Lord Richardson and Lord Baden have shot him and he is dead. So, there is no need to worry now but you must stay very, very still until Doctor Ormond says you may move. I am sorry if you are uncomfortable but we must prevail. I cannot stand to lose you when we have just become betrothed. Please, Love, lie still."

She continued frowning at him, then looked at her hand and smiled. "I thought I had a dream – a lovely dream. You really do want to marry me?"

"Oh, I do indeed! I do indeed, Love! As soon as you are well. Now, please just lie very, very still. We do not want the bleeding to start again. I am so sorry if you are not very comfortable but it will be well, you will see, it will be well!"

Ruth brought a warm coverlet; Kenneth moved his leg enough for it to cover the areas Dr. Ormond was not attending. She sighed and said that helped she was very cold. No one told her it was because she had been very close to death. Kenneth could not say the words and he imagined her parents could not as well.

Kenneth was alarmed for a second then realized Elizabeth had gone to sleep, for he could feel her heart and breathing. He had to get a grip on himself if he were to help her through this! Doctor Ormond asked him to move his hands, that he was going to sew things up and pressure was no longer needed right now, he would let him know what to do next in a few minutes. Kenneth swung his leg from where it was over her midsection and tried to stand up. Thankfully, Alfred was there to steady him or he may have fallen....both legs being numb.

"Kenneth, can we talk a minute please?" asked the Major.

"Yes, Sir!" Alfred looked around and realizing people were no longer gathered near Elizabeth he pulled up two chairs, still within close range and pointed for Kenneth to sit down.

"I am quite pleased, Kenneth, with your interest in Elizabeth and your willingness in the past two years to help her beyond expectations anyone may have had. I know your good feelings are returned by her. She had made that very clear to anyone paying attention that you are indeed the only man she is at all interested in, if her acceptance of your ring wasn't proof enough. However, today's events may have changed things somewhat. Don't look at me askance…it is just facts I am addressing. It is hard to tell what if any long-term effect such a severe injury may have on her constitution. If it leaves her sickly or otherwise incapacitated, then you may need to reconsider your proposal. Don't look at me like that! I have been through enough bodily trauma to speak from firsthand knowledge. I must warn you that things like childbirth and running a school as well as a big estate may be too much for her. I realize it is early times yet, but please consider what I have said."

"Well, Sir, I understand exactly what you are saying! But I am displeased with it, Sir! I am not one to run away from my decisions and my love for Elizabeth can transcend any difficulty either of us may encounter! I would hope, pray, and provide all care for her to ascertain nothing untoward results from today's event, but I will NOT be put off by it! I will NOT shirk any duty to care for her nor to plan the rest of my life with her – regardless of any problems from today's shooting! I thank you, Sir, to give me more credit and understand the depth of my love for Elizabeth! Good day to you, SIR!" And he rose from the chair and went to the other side of where Elizabeth lay and sat down on the floor at her side.

Ruth rushed up to Alfred. "What in the whole of Nature have you said to Kenneth! I have never seen the boy so put out! Alfred you did not warn him away from her because of today's event did you?"
"Well, my Dear, I believe I did and have been substantially put in my place for doing so. I am not certain the boy will ever forgive me, but I am very concerned that Elizabeth will not be herself after such an injury. I have seen some similar and they can have long-reaching results. I should have waited longer but I am so afraid both of these children are in for some severe disappointment from all this!"
"It is not your place, Alfred, to say such things on this the very first day of such damages. Elizabeth has not been left for days on a battlefield with no care. She has not lingered in a dirty field hospital

with unwashed bedding and minimal care or nourishment. She is not miles away from anyone who loves her and with the prospect of little recovery! She will have the best of care and nursing and no sparing of expenses in doing so. I feel you owe an apology to Kenneth, Alfred. I am most displeased with your comments to him!"

She walked away as well.

Holy Cow as Elizabeth would say he had certainly been put in his place!

About that time, Elizabeth gave a loud groan and Doctor Ormond whispered something to her and patted her other shoulder. He then asked Kenneth to help him sit her up and put more pillows behind her, which Ruth had brought evidently while he and Alfred were talking. As she was raised, Elizabeth gasped at the pain and then coughed while big tears rolled down her cheeks.

"There, there, Elizabeth, I know I have made you hurt worse, but you need to be upright for a bit. It is important that you not get pneumonia. I am having a bed brought down into this room for use tomorrow, so you do not have to move much. And your maid has been sent for by Ruth to come and bring you a nightdress and a great number of pillows and spreads. Someone will stay with you night and day for the next few days and you are to immediately tell anyone if you feel worse, if the pain is more severe than right now, or there is a dampness, such as a bleed from the wound. Do you understand that Elizabeth?"

"Yes, yes, Doctor. I do understand. I am sorry for being such a baby, but the pain is most severe! I will try to be good and I will follow your directions, I promise. Thank you Doctor for your help! I am afraid this day has kept you quite busy and not been the social outing you may have expected. I am so regretful but very thankful for your demanding work!"

"Well, well now, my Dear. No need to be regretful, I am just so very glad I was invited to this birthday party and thought to bring my bag and things – just a habit I have had – finding I am often needed unexpectedly! I have spoken with Ruth and Kenneth and they are prepared to provide all the care you may need. That is a fine young man you have there – and by the way congratulations to you both – what a beautiful ring! Keep your good future in mind and you will heal before you know it but please do not move around much for a week....I know with the school and all it will be hard but it will pay dividends in the long run. I am going to go clean up and borrow a shirt from your father – then I plan to eat some of your good birthday food, since I haven't had my nuncheon!" and with that he laughed and left the room, showing bloody signs of her issue on the front of his shirt and waistcoat.

Kenneth was holding some tea for her and she found she was indeed thirsty. She managed a smile for him and he was beside himself with pleasure! There was considerable hurrying and scurrying behind them and Elizabeth assumed it was the setting up of her bed in this new location. Several maids, including Julie, were bringing bedding, a bed warming pan, a slop jar, a basin and towels with a stand for them and many other things. It looked like the ball room was now going to be an over-sized bedroom for her…well, so be it! Big Jim stopped by her floor position and told her he would be spending the night in the adjoining room, in the event she needed to be moved in the night and therefore providing Kenneth with help. She was aghast that Kenneth would be doing so but got a similar lecture from her betrothed to what her father had gotten – about his caring for her.

Ruth was standing near and smiling and nodding her head – so evidently she approved the unconventional situation! Then Kenneth's mother came up and said she was pleased he was to stay and would have some clothes sent as soon as she got home.

Well, tarnation, how about that…they were all conspiring to have him stay…Very nice indeed! She couldn't have asked for more but it surprised her that it was to come about!

CHAPTER TWENTY

By the time it was an actual bedtime, Elizabeth was in considerable pain. The laudanum given by Doctor Ormond before he left had worn off and her chest felt like a horse had kicked her – maybe multiple times! However, true to his constant attention, Kenneth came with another dose and some sweet tea to help it go down. Sweet tea was a help but my goodness the medicine stuff was nasty….she was glad no regular foods tasted this bad or Ruth would fuss even more about her losing weight, because she could not tolerate such taste on a regular basis. Trying valiantly not to gag, she got the evening dose down and with cushions to keep the torn shoulder higher than her waist, per Dr. Ormond orders, she realized she was tired. She hadn't done anything for hours but it must be the toll on her body for she was going to sleep even though she would have liked to talk with Kenneth some more.

She heard some murmuring and realized Big Jim had come in to check if she needed to be moved and Kenneth told him the doctor had said for her to continue lying still where she was on the quilts on the floor for this night. She would be moved to the bed in the morning or maybe the next day if she was not visibly bleeding from the wound at that time. After assuring Kenneth would call him if needed, Jim returned to the next-door room.   Kenneth adjusted an old child's mattress, that staff had brought from the attic, beside her and using a bedspread and small pillow made himself as comfortable as a very tall man could be on a child size bed.

Elizabeth lay thinking of the two men waiting on her tonight.   How lucky could any girl get…the best employee and the best fiancé.   Jim (Big Jim as she had called him since she was a child) was the most devoted servant.   He had a pretty wife and two children but when needed at the main house he was always here.   From helping to nurse her Mother before she passed, helping to nurse her father when brought back from the army hospital and now standing by in case she needed anything.   A truly remarkable man! Not to mention his help at the school! She felt very guilty that she knew very little about his childhood or family other than his current one on this estate….seemed like her mother had once mentioned he was orphaned, something about his mother dying in childbirth – not for him but a sibling maybe.   And his father, she believed, was deceased but she couldn't remember why.   Very poor of her indeed.   Here the wonderful man had tended to her for YEARS and she didn't know much about him at all…she would correct that as soon as she could. Maybe father or mother knew.   When mother was still Aunt Ruth, she had been in and out of this house for years…perhap she knew something. On that reflective note, Elizabeth blessedly went to sleep.

Kenneth was exhausted but could not relax enough to shut his eyes. He watched his precious girl sleep and prayed – prayed that she healed well and quickly – prayed that they would have a long life together – prayed his thanks for bringing her into his life – well….just prayed!
Sometime in the night he heard a rustling and looking up there stood Jim, watching Elizabeth sleep. He grinned and pointed to the door and the two men went into the hall. "I see you can't sleep either. How long have your known Elizabeth?"

"I came to work as a young man and she was just a small girl of maybe two or three, I can't remember exactly which of those birthdays she celebrated then. But what a wonderful child she was….very much as she is now, which is odd given all the things that have passed in her life. The poor child! Her mother and father loved her but of course he was away most all of her life on military assignments and her mother – well, she was an odd one! I do not mean to be critical but she was a recluse and therefore Elizabeth, or Ellie as she was usually called, was not allowed to venture out to a regular school until quite old and had virtually no friends her own age. Just stuck here with staff, the animals, and a very unusual and reclusive mother. She wasn't even provided nice children's stories and books, except what her Aunt Ruth gave her. And when she did request something, which was a rarity, she was frequently refused – like piano lessons, visits to London, and story books. I never could figure out what her Mother was attempting by keeping the child so restricted…maybe afraid, I just don't know. But hasn't she turned out to be a marvelous person! A lot of credit goes to Ruth, of course, she has been wonderful in doing all the informative things Elizabeth wanted – ever since the untimely death of Madeline Masters when Ellie was eight."

"I know you have seen her ride and I can still remember when Ruth introduced her to riding the same year Madeline died. She took to it like a duck to water and never looked back. The animals all seemed to try their best to be good with her….almost like they understood her gentle ways and interest in them….maybe they did!"

Kenneth chuckled. "She can ride, for sure and certain! One of my first memories was at a visit to our estate by her accompanied by Ruth at some function my mother was having. She approached my father's horse, a very spirited but intelligent animal, and asked the groom if she could ride him. The groom was aghast since no member of our family ever road that beast…my father being the only one with whom the horse communicated. However, she was insistent and when Father came into the barn he suggested she be allowed to mount him in the small, enclosed ring. He stood beside her and low and behold the horse bowed his head and nickered softly at her! Father talks of it to this day! She had limited experience at that time, having just learned to ride that year, but up she went and the horse was pleased....now I see how you are looking at me...how is a horse pleased, you ask? Well, he went through the minimal paces more gently than any horse ever. Father is still amazed and loves to tell the story of how she tamed his spirited mount the very first time she was in saddle on him!"

"I can understand that. They understand her and she them! It is uncanny. Have you seen her around the hog yard? Even the most fierce sow will come to the fence and not stomp or huff or threaten....amazing! Well, I better get some sleep, she will be hurting in the morning and it will take both of us to help her...Good night, Lord Thompson."

"Oh, Jim, please call me Ken! I do not stand on formalities – nor does my father!"

"Thank you, Sir. Ken it is!"

She didn't know where she was....it was terrifying...Someone was trying to get her and she couldn't run! She whimpered and thrashed about but someone was holding her and preventing her escape...oh, help, help me! She finally took a big breath and let out a scream!   Then she was being kissed – kissed – how very strange, who would imprison her and then try to kiss her? Who was she, where was she....oh Lord help me!   Finally, someone was whispering in her ear. "Elizabeth love, wake up, wake up. You are all right, Love! I have you, no one will hurt you!"

She shuddered and tried to open her eyes but was afraid of what she would see...who was there, who had hurt her so badly....her chest was killing her...it hurt worse than anything she had ever experienced....well at least she thought so...who was she...what had they done to her?

Then she suddenly knew Kenneth was there. She clung to him with every ounce of strength she had. "Save me, save me, I am so very hurt...can you save me?"

"Yes, Love, I will save you. Here let me wipe your tears."

Using a warm rag brought by a running Julie, Kenneth wiped her face and then kissed her again...Well, that was nice. But where in tarnation was she? Not her bed certainly...much too hard and not her bedroom either...much to light. Oh, Lord, what is happening? She squeezed her eyes closed and then took a big breath...oh that was nice, cologne like Kenneth's. Finally, she managed to open her eyes. Yes, Kenneth was there, oh God, thank you!

Kenneth would save her! She clung to him until her chest hurt something awful. He was gently easing her arms from his neck and trying to get her to lay down...but she didn't want to...she wanted out of here...she wanted her bedroom!

"Hush, Darling! You have been hurt and you must not move so much. I am here and I will not leave you! I will be right here. Can you look at me, Dearest?"

She opened her eyes a little and looked straight at Kenneth...oh, thank heaven! It *is* Kenneth, but what is he doing in her bed? Well, maybe not her bed – something is awfully hard and she is very cold...not at all like the fireplace in her bedroom that Julie stoked each morning before her bath nor the grand feather mattress Ruth had bought her when she got her double bed. Just then Kenneth covered her with a warmed coverlet...ah, that was nice. All right, maybe she wasn't being attacked. Kenneth would not let anyone attack her – but she WAS injured she was certain something was terribly wrong with her chest and shoulder!

"Lie still Sweetheart, you will do injury to yourself by moving about. Dr. Ormond said for you to be as still as possible. I will stay here beside you. Would you like some tea?" She nodded her head but evidently that wasn't such a good idea because it made her chest and shoulder hurt more.

"Kenneth, what has happened to me? I hurt something awful. I don't believe I went riding, did I? If a horse threw me it would indeed be unusual…for I have never had one do so, or I don't believe I have…I am not too certain of things right now."

Kenneth chuckled. "Well, you were not thrown by a horse but you were shot in the chest yesterday."

"Oh, quit teasing me, Kenneth. Shot? Who in the world would shoot me during my birthday party and why for pity sake? It was my birthday wasn't it?"

"Yes, Dear. We are only guessing at the why, but the "who", is the man who shot at you yesterday and nicked your father instead. An incompetent deputy let him escape and he came back and tried to kill you again. He shot you just below the shoulder in the chest. So, you MUST lie very still, Dearest. You must not thrash about. Dr. Ormond has the majority of the bleeding in hand right now but we don't want the injury opened again. You must help us, Sweetheart. You must lie very still and let Jim and I attend you. Now it is daylight, I expect your parents to be here soon, too. Jim and I have attended you all night and you did get some good sleep. It is very important that you listen to all instructions. It was an awful wound. You must take great care. The good thing is it didn't hit a lung or your heart but it did considerable damage otherwise. Here let me give you another drink of the tea and then it will soon be time for more medicine. Perhaps they will bring some gruel too. I will not leave you. But you must agree to rest and stay as still as possible. Do you promise to do so?"

"Yes, Kenneth, I promise. This is all so confusing. Is it true that the man shot father because he wanted to shoot me? Just because his worker went to the school and got a better job?"

"That's it exactly, Dear! At least as far as we know from what he shouted. The worker got a better position because of your good teachings and left the scoundrel with no one to take in his crops, which I understand were meagre at best...but he was trying to lay the blame elsewhere as do so many who are lazy and inept. Now, enough of this. Please lay very still and we will wait for your parents to arrive then get more nourishment into you. Mother knows I will stay until you are much better so I will be helping take care of you. I am strong enough to lift you, as is Jim and your Mother or Julie are not. You must not move about. If you need your chamber pot, let me know and I will assist you onto it and Julia will attend you...do not give me that look of alarm...you are most injured and hospital rules will apply...you must have help doing anything that involves moving until the chest can heal a little. You almost bled to death, my dearest girl, so you MUST be very, very careful!"

274

Well, tarnation! How about that! He would help her onto the chamber pot? He would attend her – he and evidently Jim as well. How embarrassing! But she doubted Ruth, being very small in stature, or Julie either, could lift her as tall as she is, oh my, she was humiliated beyond belief! "Kenneth, what if he comes back, what if he injures someone else, oh dear, what can we do?"

"Hush don't get yourself upset. He cannot return. Lords Baden and Richardson have shot him and he is dead. They followed him immediately after you were shot and together finished him off. If they stand for the assizes, there are any number of us to testify. Do not worry yourself at all!"

Well, that was astounding! They had shot him dead? She guessed she wasn't surprised, Lord Richardson being a military man and Lord Baden having survived attempts on his life a few years back....her heroes now! As she snuggled into the quilts, Elizabeth was more comfortable than she would have thought she could be. Kenneth had fluffed the pillows and folded another coverlet and by gently turning her got it under as more of a mattress. She went back to sleep with Kenneth laying on a small cot beside her and holding her hand. Just as she drifted off, she realized the medicine must have laudanum in it.

Kenneth watched her and wondered what the outcome from such a serious shot would have on her life. It was known that mini-balls and bullets often caused infections and other serious problems...he could only hope that would not be the case. He had noticed that Dr. Ormond used considerable whiskey as a wash to the wound, and it was good for sanitizing. They would face it together, whatever occurred, but it was certainly scary. He had never been in a position to worry about anyone else like this. His younger brother had been ill with a fever but by five days later was as good as new. He had all four grandparents still alive and active considering their ages – he just wasn't used to anyone he loved needing nursing...well, he would get used to it. She would not want for a thing...he would see to that for sure and certain!

Neither had noticed Ruth at the door during the last bit of Kenneth's speech to Elizabeth. She was smiling to herself – although of course very worried. But Elizabeth was in good hands. Doctor Ormond was excellent as proven by his care of Alfred when returned from the awful army hospital. She had watched him many times and realized unlike some doctors he was aware of infection and that it could be prevented if careful and he seemed to know how to stitch to hold a wound and all with the utmost cleanliness. Things were as good as they could be, she supposed. She tiptoed to Kenneth and whispered would he like her to bring him some breakfast and he smiled and nodded.

Elizabeth was sleeping and seemed to be as comfortable as could be expected. The next four or five days would be very painful, he was certain...a gunshot wound was hard to heal. He would have loved to have been in on the chase for the man but thankfully the guys had succeeded in eliminating him for good!
There was considerable noise in the hall and he went out quietly, shutting the door tightly behind him. "Gentlemen, you must be quiet. Elizabeth is sleeping and in much pain when she is awake. I will not tolerate such noise. Please take your discussion outside if you must speak so loudly!"

He noticed a man in uniform with a badge and assumed it was the sheriff. He approached him and said: "I wish to speak with you but cannot leave Elizabeth right now, however, you WILL hear from me. It is unconscionable that a felon who had already injured one of our party, was allowed to return and has now almost killed my fiancé! You will be brought up on charges of incompetence at my earliest convenience. Now, if you must talk in such a voice as is heard in gambling houses – DO IT OUTSIDE! Mistress Masters is trying to sleep and in severe straights from your incompetence…I will not have her disturbed."

Alfred was just descending the stairs and wanted to applaud but decided no further noise would be tolerated by Kenneth. He motioned for the sheriff to follow him and they went out the back door.

CHAPTER TWENTY-ONE

Doctor Ormond returned the next day as he had promised. They had not moved Elizabeth yet from her floor position, because she seemed to be sleeping off the morning medicine well and they dd not want to wake her. For when she was awake she was in so very much pain that it was to be avoided if possible. The good doctor gently removed the bandage and examined the wound, not touching it much but looking carefully at it and at the staining on the bandage. "I am most pleased Master Kenneth. It looks better than I would have hoped, evidently you have succeeded in keeping her quiet and unmoved. If she will cooperate, please try to get her to stay in this position another day. It is not that I am displeased but the exact opposite. It looks calm and much less bleeding than I would have imagined. Her position is exactly correct if it can be maintained a while longer. I see you have added more padding underneath her body and that is fine as long as the shoulder is steady and slightly elevated as now.

I will return tomorrow morning again and we may move her to a bed at that time. Keep up the good work, My Man! Kept it up!" Whereupon he applied a new bandage and gave them the old one to burn. Ruth had been standing near and thanked the Doctor profusely. "What may she have to eat or drink, Doctor, providing she wants anything?"

"Food is not that important although hearty broth, custards, and such would be good. It is very necessary that she have liquids such as water, tea, lemonade and so forth. If rag padding can be added to her bedding then she will not need to rise for the "comfort" chair or powder room…which for another couple days would be advantageous. As I mentioned to Master Kenneth. Try to convince her of that if you will. I realize she may be embarrassed but make her understand any movement needs to be curtailed. No changing of clothes, bathing or walking about! I should return about this same time tomorrow."

"She is a most fortunate girl. The bullet did much less damage than the location would indicate and she is young and healthy. How it avoided breaking a bone or entering a major artery or her heart I do not know – the Lord moves in mysterious ways as the hymn says. She should repair very well and quickly but she must be most cautious while the place is healing as severe bleeding could still occur. When she awakes, please give her my best regards. I will be by sometime tomorrow. Good Day!"

Ruth saw Kenneth frowning and asked him what was the matter?

Kenneth sighed. "Well, the news was as good as could be expected. She would probably object to not

280

using a comfort chair but I will get her to thinking better about that and I will stay and lay beside her so I can make certain she has anything available for her every waking moment."

As Ruth nodded, he asked didn't they have a medicine cup with the long spout? Ruth frowned and said she thought she remembered one used for Madeline and maybe for Alfred too but would have to look – maybe it had gotten broken. He indicated he felt it would be easier to get more liquid for her to drink that way than holding her head at such a stiff angle for a regular cup without spilling it on her or moving the injured shoulder. He believed his grandmother had one if Ruth could not find one here. Ruth went to immediately find Julia, who had been on staff this whole number of years – they would do a thorough search right away! As Julia was asked about the medicine pitcher, she frowned and then smiling ran from the room. Shortly thereafter she was back. "This needs a good washing but I believe this is what you seek" And she was indeed holding the small pitcher with the elongated spout.

"Wherever did you find it?"

"In Elizabeth's old toy chest. I remembered she had tried to feed the kitten with it right after her Father got so he didn't need it anymore. And sure, and certain there it was with the old toys! I'll go clean it well and be right back!"

Having heard the conversation, Kenneth laughed. "I can just see her trying to get the kitten to drink from that! Of course, since they lap rather than drink it was a lost effort but I bet it would have been cute to watch her!"

"Well, Kenneth from your attentiveness and engagement I assume you would think anything she did was attractive, but you are probably right – I doubt the kitten took to it kindly though!" and laughing she went toward the kitchen.

Kenneth was pleased to see that all the talking had not seemed to bother Elizabeth's sleep. She sighed on occasion but didn't frown or fuss in her sleep – therefore he hoped she wasn't in much pain.

Ruth returned from the kitchen with some meat and fried potatoes and a piece of raisin cake. He thanked her as he also drank heavily from the lemonade and said he would stay and keep watch. He couldn't bear to move away.

Realizing he was quite tired after finishing the food, he rearranged his small mattress, pillow and blanket and lay beside his sweet girl and went to sleep immediately, holding her hand.

Several people checked on them not the least of which was Jim and Alfred but no one said a word so as not to disturb the two young people asleep on the floor. Feeling the house was a bit chilly, Ruth gently spread another cover over them both and it didn't seem to disturb them in the least. Tiptoeing away, she let staff know to spread the word to not enter the room or disturb the two as they slept. She herself decided it would be a good time to rest as well, it certainly had not been the great birthday celebration they had hoped for "their girl"! Taking a crocheted throw, she lay down on the settee, being so short it made plenty of bed and would allow her to hear if Elizabeth needed anything.

Alfred was so relieved to see his precious child resting well and also that Ruth was asleep, for she had been too stressed in the night to get much rest. He decided it was a good time to also nap and telling Jim, as he passed him in the next room, that he was going up to bed – he did so.

All of the staff were abuzz with the terrible time and awful ending to what was to be a grand birthday celebration. Elizabeth was engaged to that handsome boy who had attended to the school fixings so well. How nice! He would make her a good husband – he knew how to work and in their estimation that counted for a lot!

Household staff stationed themselves in areas that would have access to the room where the young people rested – so as to thwart any person trying to enter and maybe disturb them. The cooks were fixing anything they could think of that would be easily drunk and nourishing for Elizabeth and also preparing a roast with browned potatoes and several vegetables for "that young man", Alfred and Ruth to have for their supper when they awakened. One of the girls heated milk and melted a chocolate she had kept as a prize for herself. She explained that her mother's favorite drink was warm milk with chocolate melted in it. Maybe Dear Elizabeth would like it as well.

Jim spent his time close at hand still but reflecting on anything Elizabeth might need or want for the next session of the school. He assumed it would again be well attended and had been impressed with the number of local estate staff who had come for education in up-to-date farming and orchard classes. The courses in naval operations, mathematics, mapping, literature and grammar had of course been well attended and would enable some students to achieve an invitation to schools of higher learning but he was the most interested in how great the whole educational process had been for local people to do better at their jobs or even acquire a better position. He smiled when he thought of the poor rag-a-muffin child who had attended the first day and within this two 5-month sessions learned so very much he could now assist Doctor Ormond. That alone was sufficient achievement to make the school worthwhile.

Jim started with a jerk when a hand patted him on the shoulder. Kenneth grinned and motioned for them to go outside, he had a full pot of tea and two cups with him. As they exited the back door, they shared the tea and Kenneth said Ruth was attending Elizabeth and noticed Jim wasn't asleep. "What do you think will happen with such a wound as Elizabeth has?" the boy asked. "Well, I don't know much about gun wounds except they can have problems greater than an injury when building or thrown by a horse. Something about the gunpowder being present or the casing causing a problem. However, Dr. Ormond really cleaned the wound well with whiskey and that alone may be the thing that keeps it from becoming septic. I have seen that done with wounds created by a very dirty board or horse hoof and it seems to usually work. I'm not certain I understand why but evidently the alcohol somehow kills whatever foreign matter is left behind in the wound. Very strange if you ask me! It looks like if it kills anything it would injure the tissue but according to Dr. Ormond when I questioned him it doesn't work that way…the tissue isn't injured – just any foreign matter. Surgery is really scary, so often the patient dies even when attended by a very good doctor – but Ormond is renowned for bringing his patients back to good health. What do you think?"

"I really do not know either. A friend is in medical school and has told me of the increased use of various kinds of distilled alcohol to clean instruments and wounds. It all sounds strange but if it works all the better in each case. I certainly pray it will prevent Elizabeth from any further troubles."

"What possesses a person to be so evil? To want to kill a beautiful and caring young woman who has only tried to help people? Makes one think that evil is prevalent and not always explainable."

"Well, I agree wholeheartedly. To hurt someone like Elizabeth Masters is indeed evil of the worst kind. How about pouring me some more of that tea before it is too tepid and we will go shortly and look about our girl again."

CHAPTER TWENTY-TWO

What a two weeks! Elizabeth was sitting on the patio with chicken soup and caramel flan. With the sun on her back and really feeling quite the thing. She, of course, couldn't move her arm without considerable pain still, but the rest of her was quite all right. She had been sleeping in the bed they set up for her, after the first three nights, thankfully not on the hard floor anymore and her precious Kenneth had left this morning to check on his job and his parents – the first time he had left her since she was shot, having slept on a single bed beside her every night.

Elizabeth had promised to help little Jimmie with his reading this afternoon. Although his mother was chagrined that he would bother her, Elizabeth assured her it was a pleasure to help him. He would also do a slate full of number problems she would devise and the only ones he usually missed were division – although most of those were correct as well. She didn't feel there was ever any student more interested in learning nor more capable for that matter. Even Kenneth had given him things to read and thought problems to work out, knowing the boy was unusually smart. She could not write properly with her injured arm but he wrote out what she instructed and together they had a good school of one.

She heard the door and her parents came out with plates of food. "May we eat with you, Dear?"

"Oh, how lovely. I was just toying with my food and thinking of Jimmie. It will be nice to have someone to eat with so I don't miss Kenneth so much. Here put your plates on this table, the weather is divine! Not at all the rainy solemn weather England so often has this time of year. Look at my recent bouquet. Bless his heart, Jimmie is a quick learner so I will need to show him how to pick flowers with enough stem to reach the water in the cup. What a dear child he is – such a delight!"

"I have failed shamefully to not be asking you Mother how you are feeling. Is your pregnancy giving you any sickness and you are well?"

"Oh, yes, Dear. I am quite the thing. Not ill or inconvenienced in any way. I am so very excited though."

Ellie noticed her father looked a little green. So, she laughed and asked after him.

"I am beyond pale, Darling. I really am. My sweet Ruth is fine but I am more than worried and concerned about what is to come! And it has been such a very long time since I have handled a baby! What if I injure the child with only my one arm to use? What if the child is afraid of me or I can't provide the care I should?"

"Oh, for Heaven's sake, Father! You are a wonderful man and the baby will be fine. You will not drop the child and will provide loving care – which is really all a child needs, you know. Just to be loved! Plus, we have such great staff to assist with everything. It will be well…you will see!"

"Now there is something of consequence I need to discuss with you both. I wish to get married as soon as my shoulder heals. I see you looking askance. But I do and that is a fact. I have agreed with Kenneth before he left today and he will talk with his parents this week. He will also organize his work, arrange for his final attorney test and then be ready to marry. Father you are not looking so well…please agree with me on this! By the time Kenneth's things are worked out my arm should be virtually healed except for exercises, with which Doctor Ormond assures me he will assist. I will be nineteen by then. We have had several large parties, your wedding, several of my birthdays and of course the first year of the school. I do NOT want a big wedding and reception! I know it is done but I don't want it. Call me gun shy or whatever you want but I really want my wedding to be an intimate affair with just mostly family and a few very close friends like the Badens. I would like staff to attend instead of having to provide food and a party for everyone else. The minister can come here, it does not have to be in the church to be reverent."

It will not be immediately, of course. I want this shoulder in better condition and as stated, Kenneth has several things to finish and arrange. However, in the meantime, we need to get him a proper office here. I had thought a building addition on the east side to the back with a lot of windows and a private entrance might be just the thing – a surprise for him. I will have another complete school year to finish as well. Now that the school is better organized, I plan to hire more staff to handle student work assistance and food serving, a school principal, plus additional people in the kitchen, which will be enlarged. It is time I use some of my wealth to keep from putting a burden on those who have helped me through the years!

As to you two – well, I know you may like to move to your own home, but please know I would love to have you both here always as would Kenneth. So, it will be up to you what you decide. I will not take offense if you decide the Glass Castle is not where you want to live with your family. I will gladly deed you acreage to build here if that is your wish or will understand if you move elsewhere. Ruth your house is lovely and I do not want to influence you in any way – but a place with horses for you both would be nice and more rooms so you have live-in servants and so forth too. Whatever YOU decide is fine with me but know both Kenneth and I would be most happy if you choose to live here – either in this house or building one on this property. Just because I will inherit all my wealth in less than three years does not mean you must leave!"

"Oh, My Darling Girl! How generous you are and so accommodating. However, between us we have a virtual fortune, thanks to your Mother and the good handling of our financial people. We had thought to buy about fifty hectare of land and start building this summer. There is some available land just down the road between here and Ruth's house and we would be close but not under foot. Does that sound all right with you? Large enough for horses but not like a farm that takes a lot of tending. It would be close enough for our children to be connected and to keep in touch. We would attend the same church but be 'on our own' so to speak. You have been so wonderful dear Elizabeth, since the first I came to visit you and Madeline, so I would like the closeness but I would not feel I was 'under foot' as the saying goes." Said Ruth.

"That sounds perfect. Close enough I can ride down to visit and see you at church and you can come up here on occasion. Very nice! Our children can be friends as well as related. That is wonderful! Do you have plans you will share? I am excited to see what you are going to build."

291

"Well, we will let you see them. Right now, they are getting some things redrawn but the architect should have them back to us next week. Are you planning any changes here? I know this is a huge house but do you have any plans?"

"Yes, indeed I do. As a surprise for Kenneth, an office complex for him with lots of light and high ceilings for all his library of legal books and such. The room will get the morning light, which should please him because he is an early riser and I calculate he will start his workday early. Plus, a small stable for his and his client's horses. Does that sound good to you?"

"Oh, it sounds exactly right!"

"Well, let us eat our lunches, we plan to ride afterward, while I still can mount a horse comfortably, and we will leave you to teach your student. Thank you, Darling Elizabeth for your love and generosity. I know you and Kenneth will be most happy – you deserve each other!"

That evening as the sun set, Elizabeth reflected on her life and how extremely happy she was – chest injury notwithstanding. "Thank you God!" she prayed.

THE END

1800's DATA – *"The Era of Enlightenment"*

*A "stone" as used in various text from this period was a weight measurement of about fourteen (14) pounds as we now use.

*Hectare – about 2.471 Acres – and is a metric measurement

*Firearms were expensive as was ammunition. The armies of the day had cannon, rifles, and handguns but these were difficult and expensive to obtain by most individuals. All were reloaded after one shot.

*Estates, as used herein, were vast and virtual villages with many workers of various skills. Often entire families lived and worked there. Fortunate ones were on estates such as the Glass Castle or Summerwood, where children were educated, fair wages paid, also living and working conditions were good. Cities too had some houses or small estates with good conditions but unfortunately many people were uneducated and worked for meagre income.

*Medicine was in its infancy and some doctors bled people as a cure and few drugs were available. Doctors in these stories were the more educated and used better medical techniques, such as Dr. Ormond.

*Women as a rule had little input but many were beginning to honor those more knowledgeable. However, colleges and universities were still for male students. Women teachers, nurses, etc. gained knowledge as apprentices or were self-taught.

*Parliament – then as now – was the English governing body and very powerful.

Made in the USA
Monee, IL
09 October 2022